W9-CHT-350

Santillana
Mi primera
antología
K
Edición Anotada
Descubre el español
Santillana

Descubre el español con Santillana K
Mi primera antología Edición Anotada
ISBN-13: 9780882724935
ISBN-10: 0-88272-493-2

Published in the United States of America.

Editorial and Production Staff

Editorial Director: Mario Castro
Senior Editor: Patricia E. Acosta
Contributing Writer: María Á. Pérez
Illustrations: Maia Miller (Print Awareness), Laura González (Decoding), Sara Palacios (Reading)
Copyeditor and Proofreader: Lourdes M. Cobiella
Design and Production Manager: Mónica Candelas
Layout and Design: M. Patricia Reyes
Photo Research Editor: Mónica Candelas
Cover Design and Layout: Studio Montage

Mi primera antología is a component of *Descubre el español con Santillana*, a series conceptualized and developed by the editorial department of Santillana USA Publishing Company Inc. The publisher gratefully acknowledges the contribution of the following educators who professionally reviewed the material:

Lorena Kogan, Dual Language Immersion Teacher in Pinellas County, Florida
Colleen Wapole, Ph.D, Dual Language Immersion Teacher and Administrator in Pinellas County, Florida

Santillana USA Publishing Company Inc.
2023 NW 84th Avenue
Doral, Florida 33122
www.santillanausa.com

www.descubreelespanol.com

Printed in USA by Bradford and Bigelow, Inc.

18 17 16 15 14 2 3 4 5 6 7 8 9 10

Acknowledgments

Text: p. 24, excerpt from "El conejo" © by Isabel Freire de Matos, used by permission from Marisol Matos Freire; p. 54, adaptation of "Por si no te lo he dicho," © by Santillana Ecuador, used by permission from Santillana Ecuador

Photos: p. 150: Gary Yim / Shutterstock.com; Anthony Correia / Shutterstock.com, p. 152 - danza- Dmitry Morgan / Shutterstock.com, p. 153 - escritor - haak78 / Shutterstock.com, p. 153 - escultora - pcruciatti / Shutterstock.com

The publisher has made every effort to secure permissions for all the copyrighted reading selections, photos, and illustrations included in this book. Any errors or omissions will be corrected in future printings, as information becomes available.

Índice

Índice

Decoding

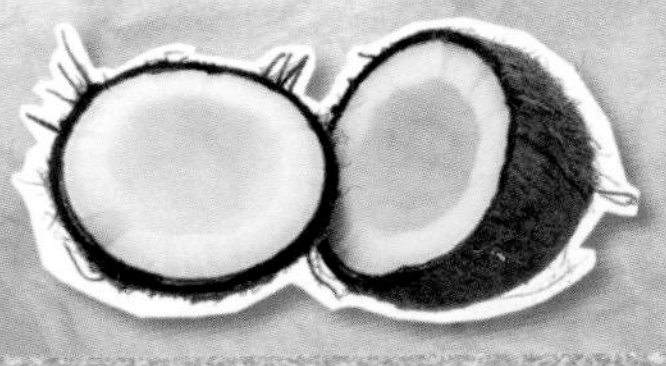

Reading

To Teachers and Parents

Descubre el español con Santillana is a comprehensive program designed to teach Spanish in elementary school classrooms. Created with teacher flexibility in mind, the program can be used in a foreign-language-in-the-elementary-school (FLES) setting, or it can be used to support Spanish-language-immersion instruction.

The **Antologías** are an integral part of *Descubre el español con Santillana.* They are a collection of authentic, grade level-appropriate literature, thematically correlated to each unit of the textbook. There is one **Antología** for each grade, K through 5.

The **Antología** for K, entitled **Mi primera antología**, includes three readings from different genres in eight thematic units, for a total of 24 readings. This allows teachers to accommodate the needs of students of Spanish as well as the needs of heritage speakers, who generally have more vocabulary resources than beginning FLES students. The reading selections are divided into three stages: Print Awareness, Decoding, and Reading. These stages are somewhat flexible, which means a teacher may choose to conduct activities suggested in the Reading stage with stories in the Decoding and Print Awareness stages as well.

Fillable PDFs have been specifically designed for this component so students can mark, draw, and write their responses. These are useful as answer sheets, referenced as such in the teacher annotations, or as consumable pages, and are available to download with the purchase of the **Edición Anotada** and the **Audio CD.** For information on how to purchase these items, please visit www.descubreelespanol.com.

Print Awareness: Before being able to decode, students should have a strong foundation in both phonological and print awareness. In **Mi primera antología**, students are introduced to letter names and shapes, syllables, and sound-spelling correspondence in order to prepare them to read words.

Decoding: When students are ready to apply their word-recognition skills and their knowledge of letter-sound relationships, they move into the stage of decoding. In **Mi primera antología**, students will recognize familiar words more quickly and they will figure out how to pronounce words they haven't seen before.

Reading: To complete the flexible yet targeted scaffolding of the reading selections, students who are ready to decode and understand words, phrases, and sentences are on their way to becoming independent readers. In **Mi primera antología**, students will find opportunities not only to decode and comprehend, but also to demonstrate comprehension of what they read.

The teacher-annotated version of **Mi primera antología**, or **Edición Anotada**, includes appropriate pre- and post-reading activities designed to help support the literacy skills taught in *Descubre el español con Santillana* Level K, including accessing prior knowledge, vocabulary, phonics, reading fluency, reading comprehension, spelling, and writing. The **Edición Anotada** contains point-of-use teaching suggestions and answer keys. This makes **Mi primera antología** an ideal tool to support children as they take their first steps in the acquisition of reading and literacy skills. The reading selections can be used for shared, guided, or independent reading. Also, the book is flexible enough to be used at home by parents as a stand-alone reading companion.

The *Common Core State Standards* (CCSS) point out that "Reading aloud allows children to experience written language…, granting them access to content that they may not be able to read or understand by themselves." The **Audio CD** contains professionally narrated recordings of the stories in **Mi primera antología** and of the engaging songs, whose lyrics are included as reading selections. This allows teachers opportunities to conduct daily read-alouds, read-alongs, and sing-alongs with their students.

How to Use *Mi primera antología*

Mi primera antología contains works of literature by a variety of renowned authors. When masters of the stature of Mexico's Amado Nervo take time to talk to children, it must be because they consider it extremely important. The book includes a wonderful poem by Nervo as well as works, adaptations, and excerpts by and from Hans Christian Andersen, Isabel Freire de Matos, and current authors such as Alma Flor Ada, Patricia E. Acosta, and others. In addition, this anthology also includes traditional children's songs, tongue twisters, poems, and rhymes from various Hispanic cultures.

Taking into consideration the important mandate from the CCSS to also include *informational texts,* and not just poetry and narratives, even in kindergarten books, **Mi primera antología** includes a biography of a Hispanic sports figure, as well as nonfiction, grade level-appropriate reading selections in the content areas of *science* and *social studies.*

The **Edición Anotada** includes questioning strategies and stimuli to frontload the highlighted vocabulary, build background, and make predictions before reading the selection. The use of appropriate reading strategies is essential for the development of reading skills. At the kindergarten level, teachers are encouraged to *read aloud* (or play the Audio CD), *echo read,* and to conduct *choral readings.* Constant re-reading is essential. In addition, having students answer simple questions while reading, or having them *retell* the story, is highly recommended.

Comprendo lo que leí

This one-page section in **Mi primera antología** includes comprehension activities designed to measure how well students understand the selection. The teacher instructions as well as the answer keys found in the **Edición Anotada** help teachers guide their students as they engage in activities that practice simple (direct recall) and *higher-order, critical-thinking skills* (usually in open-ended questions).

Así se dice

This one-page section in **Mi primera antología** focuses on phonics and spelling patterns in order to promote vocabulary development. These activities help students understand the relationship between letters and sounds, and give them opportunities to practice their penmanship skills as they begin to trace and spell letters and syllables.

Así se escribe

The focus of this section in **Mi primera antología** is for students to understand how they can express themselves by writing. These activities help students practice spelling words, applying what they have learned about sound-letter relationships. They will also learn and practice writing conventions, such as capitalization and beginning and end punctuation.

A escribir

This is another opportunity for students to engage in the critical thinking skills of analyzing and evaluating concepts and vocabulary before drawing and writing a response to a prompt related to the theme of the unit and the selection they read, or were read. Teachers may also use this as an opportunity for students to start practicing *journal writing,* and to apply what they learned and practiced in **Comprendo lo que leí, Así se dice**, and **Así se escribe**. Teachers who choose this option may want to create a booklet with students' responses to these prompts to keep as their daily journals.

Reading Comprehension Skills and Strategies

Author's Point of View

All stories have a narrator. Sometimes, the narrator is an outside observer and tells the story in the third-person, using pronouns, such as **he**, **she**, **him**, **her**, **they**, and **them**. Sometimes, the narrator is also a character in the story and uses pronouns such as **I**, **me**, **my**, and **mine**. When the narrator is an outside observer, the author is using the third-person point of view to tell the story. When the narrator is a character, the author is using the first-person point of view to tell the story. Guide students to identify pronouns in the selection that show the author's point of view.

Author's Purpose

Authors write stories for a reason. This reason is called **author's purpose**. The four main reasons for writing a story are: 1) to **inform**, or tell about something; 2) to **explain**, or describe what something is like or how something works; 3) to **entertain**, or make the reading enjoyable or funny; and 4) to **persuade**, or convince the reader to do something or to think the way the author does. Sometimes, authors have more than one purpose for writing a story. Ask students to identify the author's main purpose for writing the selection. Help them to find and name the details that the author uses to accomplish the purpose.

Cause and Effect

A **cause** is why something happens. An **effect** is what happens as a result of that cause. Sometimes, words such as **because**, **so**, **since**, **therefore**, and others, give clues to indicate cause and effect relationships in a story. However, a story may not include these words and still have cause and effect relationships. Encourage students to find any signal words that may be present in the story and help them to identify cause and effect relationships in the selection.

Comparing and Contrasting

When we tell how two or more things, events, or characters are alike, we are **comparing**. When we tell how two or more things, events, or characters are different, we are **contrasting**. Comparing and contrasting helps us to understand how people, events, or things are alike or different in a story. Have students look through the selection and help them to identify instances in which the author compares and contrasts events, characters, or things.

Drawing Conclusions

We **draw conclusions** when we take information about a character or event in a story and then make a statement, or conclusion, about that character or event based on that information. Have students look through the paragraphs they are reading and model how to draw conclusions about the characters and/or events.

Echo Reading

This reading strategy is ideal for modeling correct pronunciation and intonation of text. Start reading the selection and ask students to repeat after you. Start with words and phrases, and gradually increase to sentences. Be sure to read with emotion and in a lively manner. Avoid correcting students who mispronounce. Instead, encourage them to continue reading, following your lead, as you gradually release more responsibility to them.

Fantasy and Reality

Fantasy is something that could not happen in real life. **Reality** is everything that is real or authentic. A fantasy may be a story that includes make-believe characters such as talking animals, while a realistic story may tell about something that could happen in real life.

Help students identify stories they may know that are fantasies and stories they may know that are realistic. Ask students if the selection they are reading is realistic or if it is a fantasy. Have them identify details or examples from the selection that are make-believe or realistic.

Main Idea and Details

The **main idea** is the most important point the author makes in a story or paragraph. In a paragraph, the main idea is often contained in a topic sentence at the beginning or at the end of the paragraph. In order to support the main idea, authors use **details** in other sentences that may describe, give reasons and definitions, and give other types of information. Help students to identify the main idea and details of some of the paragraphs in the selection.

Making Inferences

We make **inferences** when we use clues from the reading and what we already know to figure out something that is not directly stated or explained in the reading. Have students make inferences about the characters or events in the selection.

Retelling

Retelling is when a reader tells the story in her or his own words. Retelling provides the reader with the opportunity to process what s/he has read by organizing and explaining it to others. Retelling can be used for a paragraph, section, or for the entire selection. Have students retell the selection by helping them to organize the events of the selection.

Sequence

Sequence is the order of events in a story. Understanding in which order events take place in a story is essential to forming ideas and opinions about a story. Words and phrases such as **first**, **then**, **finally**, **the next day**, **tomorrow**, and so on, often signal order of events and time in a story. Help students to identify order of events in the selection by having them identify time and order words or phrases.

Summarizing

When we determine the most important events or ideas in a text, we are **summarizing**. Summarizing helps us to learn how to determine essential ideas and consolidate important details that support them. Summarizing can be used with paragraphs, sections, or for the entire selection. Help students to summarize the selection by asking them to identify the most important events or ideas of the selection.

Discuss family and friends with students. Ask individual students: *¿Quién eres tú?* Who are you? *¿Quién es tu amigo o amiga?* Who is your friend? *¿Quién es tu hermano o hermana?* Who is your brother or your sister? Have students view the illustrations and help them "read" the illustrations. Ask them to predict who the characters may be. Explain that the characters are visiting Parque Nacional Patuca, a famous park in the country of Honduras.

Conoce a Ana

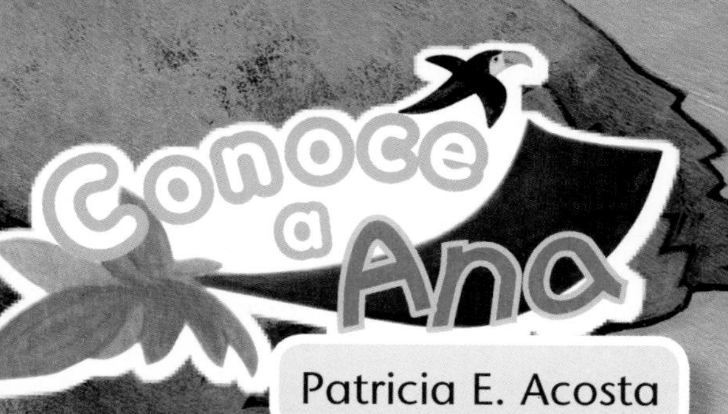

Patricia E. Acosta

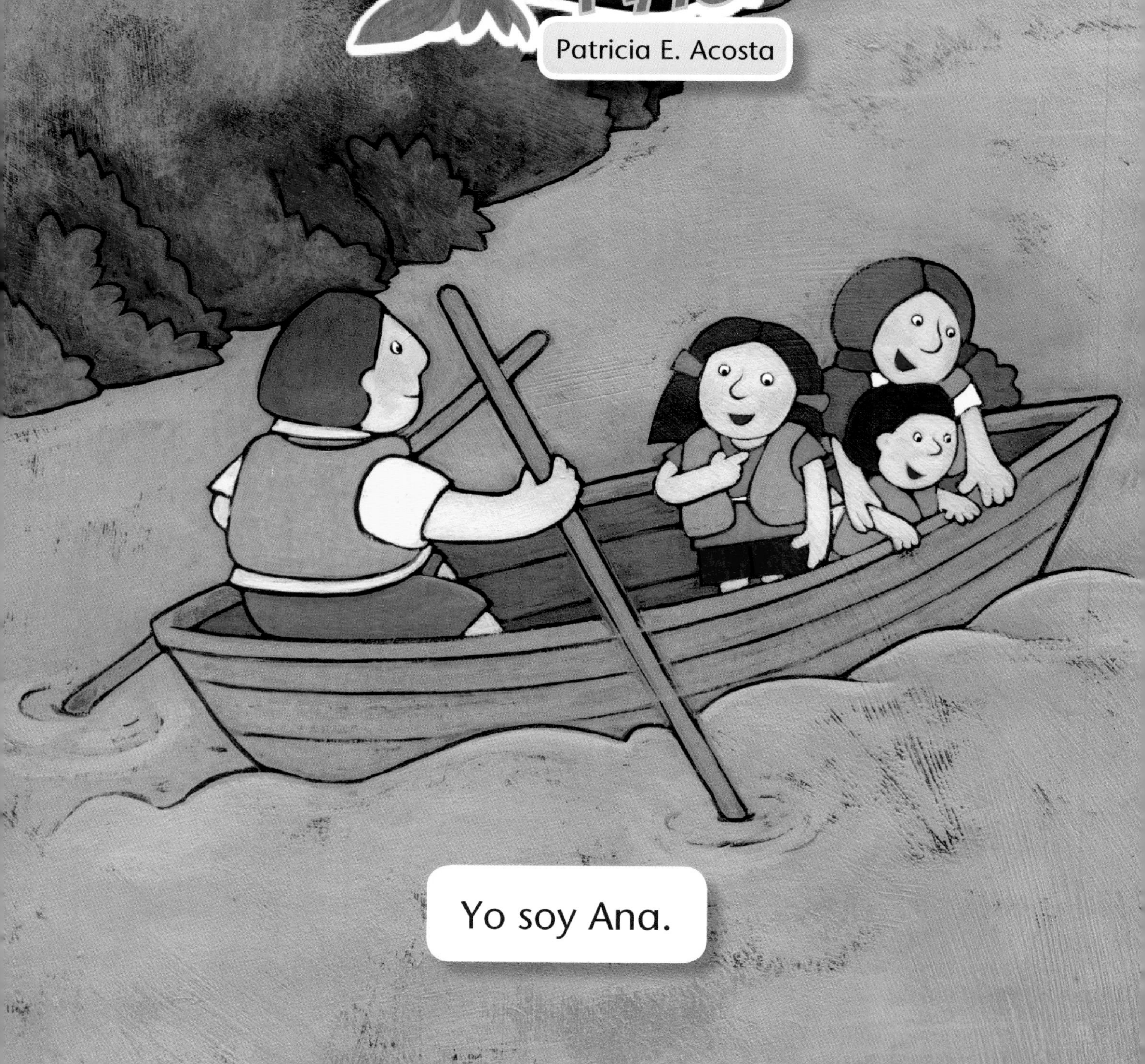

Yo soy Ana.

Explain that the words on the page represent spoken words and represent what the illustration shows. Then read the story aloud as you point to each word. Point out the space between each word and explain that you read all the words from left to right. Ask students to clap at the end of each word.

Ada es mi hermana.
Alan es mi hermano.

Read the story again and have students point to the characters as they are introduced. Discuss how the characters are related to each other. You may wish to have students illustrate and label each character. Then have students greet each character by saying hello *(¡Hola!)* and the name of the character.
Alma es mi amiga.
Aldo es mi amigo.

Comprendo lo que leí

Discuss the selection and help students complete the activities on the answer sheets. For items 1–2, have students circle the correct answer. For item 3, have students complete the sentence by writing his or her name. Then ask them to draw the main character in the story (Ana) next to him or herself.

amigo

1.  sí  no

hermano

2.  sí  no

3. Yo soy Answers will vary. . Ana es mi amiga.

Así se dice

For items 1–4, point to the pictures as you say the words *amiga, amigo, abuela,* and *abuelo.* Clarify the meaning of all words. Have students repeat after you. Then show students how to spell the letter *A a.* For items 5–6, have students read the words aloud with you as they circle the correct answer on the answer sheet.

A a

1. Aa

2. Aa

3. Aa

4. Aa

5. (amigo) abuela

6. amiga 

Así se escribe

Explain that words that name people are spelled with capital letters. For items 1–4, ask students to trace the letter that completes the word. As an extension, have students practice writing the letter *A* using noodles.

1. A na

2. a migo

3. A lan

4. a miga

A escribir

Review story vocabulary and how to spell the letter *a*. Read the question and the sentence starter. Have students write the missing letter. Then have them complete the sentence by drawing a friend.

- ¿Quién es tu amigo?

Mi a migo es  . Answers will vary.

Discuss different kinds of dwellings with students. Ask: *¿Dónde viven?* Where do you live? *¿Viven en una casa?* Do you live in a house? (Point to the house.) *¿Viven en un edificio de apartamentos?* Do you live in an apartment building? (Point to the building.) Have students view the illustrations and help them "read" them. Help students identify the kind of dwelling where the boy lives. Explain that the boy lives in an apartment building in Perú. Have students point to the title of the story. Read the title aloud and invite students to read along with you. Explain that llamas are common animals in Perú. They are used as pack animals and as a source of wool.

¿Dónde está la llama?

Patricia E. Acosta

Erik está en el edificio.

Remind students that words on a page represent spoken words and that there is a space between each word. Elicit that you read the words from left to right. Read the story slowly and ask students to tap on their desks every time you say a word.

El erizo está en la pecera.

El escarabajo está en la escalera.

Read the story again and have students talk about where the story takes place. Have students act out the story. Discuss different sources where they could learn more about dwellings or about llamas, such as the library and the Internet. Model how to search for additional illustrations and share with students.

¡Pero la llama está afuera!

Comprendo lo que leí

Discuss the selection and help students complete the activities on the answer sheets. For items 1–2, have students circle the correct answer. For item 3, have students complete the sentence by tracing the letter *e*. Then ask them to draw the apartment building where Erik lives and where the story takes place.

escalera

1.  sí  no

afuera

2.  sí  no

3. Erik vive en un e dificio.

Answers will vary.

Así se dice

For items 1–4, point to the pictures as you say the words *edificio, escritorio, erizo* and *elefante*. Clarify the meaning of all words. Have students repeat after you. Then show students how to spell the letter *E e*. For items 5–6, have students read the words aloud with you as they circle the correct answer on the answer sheet.

E e

1. 

2. E e

3. 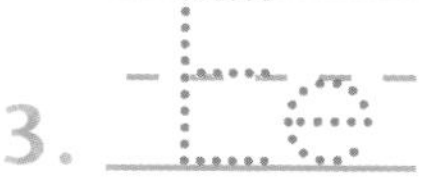

4. E e

5. edificio escalera

6. elefante 

Así se escribe

Review that people's names are spelled with capital letters. For items 1–4, ask students to trace the letter that completes the word. As an extension, have students practice writing the letter *E* using shaving cream.

1. Erik

2. elefante

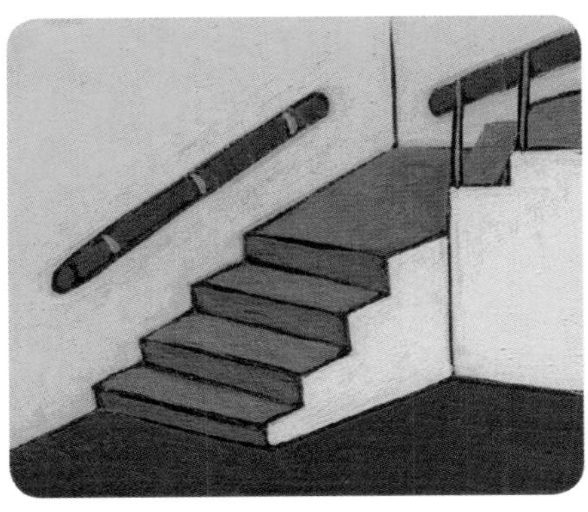

3. escalera

4. escritorio

A escribir

Review story vocabulary and how to spell the letter *e*. Read the question and the sentence about Erik, and have students complete it by writing the missing letter. Then read the sentence starter and have students complete it by drawing a house or a building, depending on where they live.

- ¿Dónde vivimos?

Erik vive en un edificio.

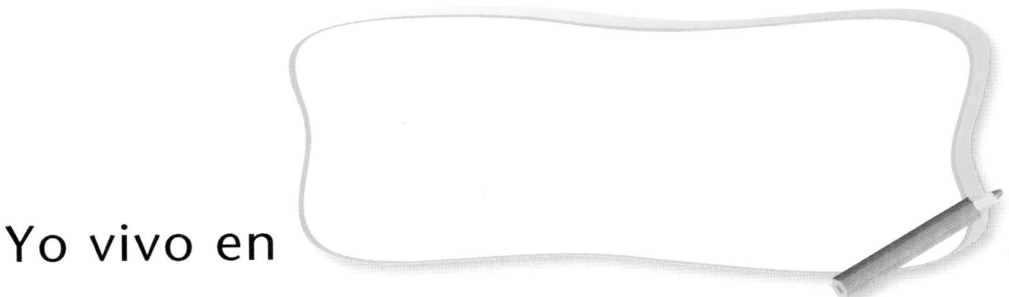

Yo vivo en ______. Answers will vary.

Discuss school locations and school subjects. Ask: *¿Dónde está su escuela?* Where is your school? *¿Qué aprenden en la escuela?* What do you learn in school? Have students view the illustrations and help them "read" them. Ask students to point to the title. Read it aloud and have students read along with you. Explain that the Dominican Republic is part of an island. Discuss what an island is.

Una escuela en la isla

Patricia E. Acosta

Los niños están en la escuela.

La escuela está en la isla.

Read the text several times. Ask students to tap their noses every time you read a word. Then have them notice how those words come together to form sentences. Have students repeat after you as you read each sentence.

Los niños aprenden en la escuela.

Los niños aprenden español.

Read the story again and help students make life-to-text connections by talking about their own school experiences and relating them to important ideas in the text. Elicit ways students could find more information about schools and about the Dominican Republic, such as from the teacher, friends, or the Internet.

Los niños aprenden inglés.

Los niños de la isla aprenden en la escuela.

Comprendo lo que leí

Discuss the selection and help students complete the activities on the answer sheets. For items 1–2, have students circle the correct answer. For item 3, have students mark with an X the pictures that show important ideas from the story.

isla

aprenden

1. sí no

2. sí no

3.

X

not marked

X

Así se dice

For items 1–4, point to the pictures as you say the words *isla*, *insecto*, *iguana*, and *imán*. Clarify the meaning of all words. Have students repeat after you. Then show students how to spell the letter *I i*. For items 5–6, have students read the words aloud with you as they circle the correct answer on the answer sheet.

I i

1. I i

2. I i

3. I i

4. I i

5. inglés 

6. español 

Así se escribe

Explain that naming words are the words that we give to things, people, animals, and places. Read the sentences and have students trace the letter that completes each naming word. As an extension, have students practice writing the letter *I* using rice.

1. Los n_i_ños de la _i_sla aprenden en la escuela.

2. Aprenden _i_nglés y español.

A escribir

Review story vocabulary and how to spell the letters *a* and *i*. Read the question and the first sentence, and have students complete it by writing the missing letters. Then read the sentence starter and have them complete the sentence by drawing another activity they do at school.

- ¿Qué aprenden los niños en la escuela?

Los niños _a_prenden _i_nglés y español.

Yo aprendo _____.

Answers will vary.

Discuss pets and other animals with students. Help students describe their favorite animal. Ask: *¿Qué animal les gusta?* Which animal do you like? *¿Cómo es el animal?* What does the animal look like? Point to the title as you read it aloud, inviting students to read along with you. Then have students view the illustrations and help them "read" them. Ask students to describe the rabbit in the pictures. Explain that it is a Spanish Giant rabbit, one of the largest breeds of rabbits in the world.

El conejo

Isabel Freire de Matos

fragmento

Read the text aloud once. Then have students chorally read along with you. Repeat the procedure and have students jump like rabbits every time a word is read. Encourage them to point to the rabbit's body parts. Emphasize the *o* sound of the highlighted words.

Mira mis orejas,
mi suave rabito,

Discuss how some words end with similar sounds. Read the story again and have students listen for rhyming words (*rabito, hociquito*). Review vocabulary and encourage students to describe the main character in the poem (the rabbit) using the highlighted words.

mis ojos redondos

y mi hociquito.

Comprendo lo que leí

Discuss the selection and help students complete the activities on the answer sheets. For items 1–2, have students circle the correct answer. For item 3, have students circle the three pictures that describe the rabbit.

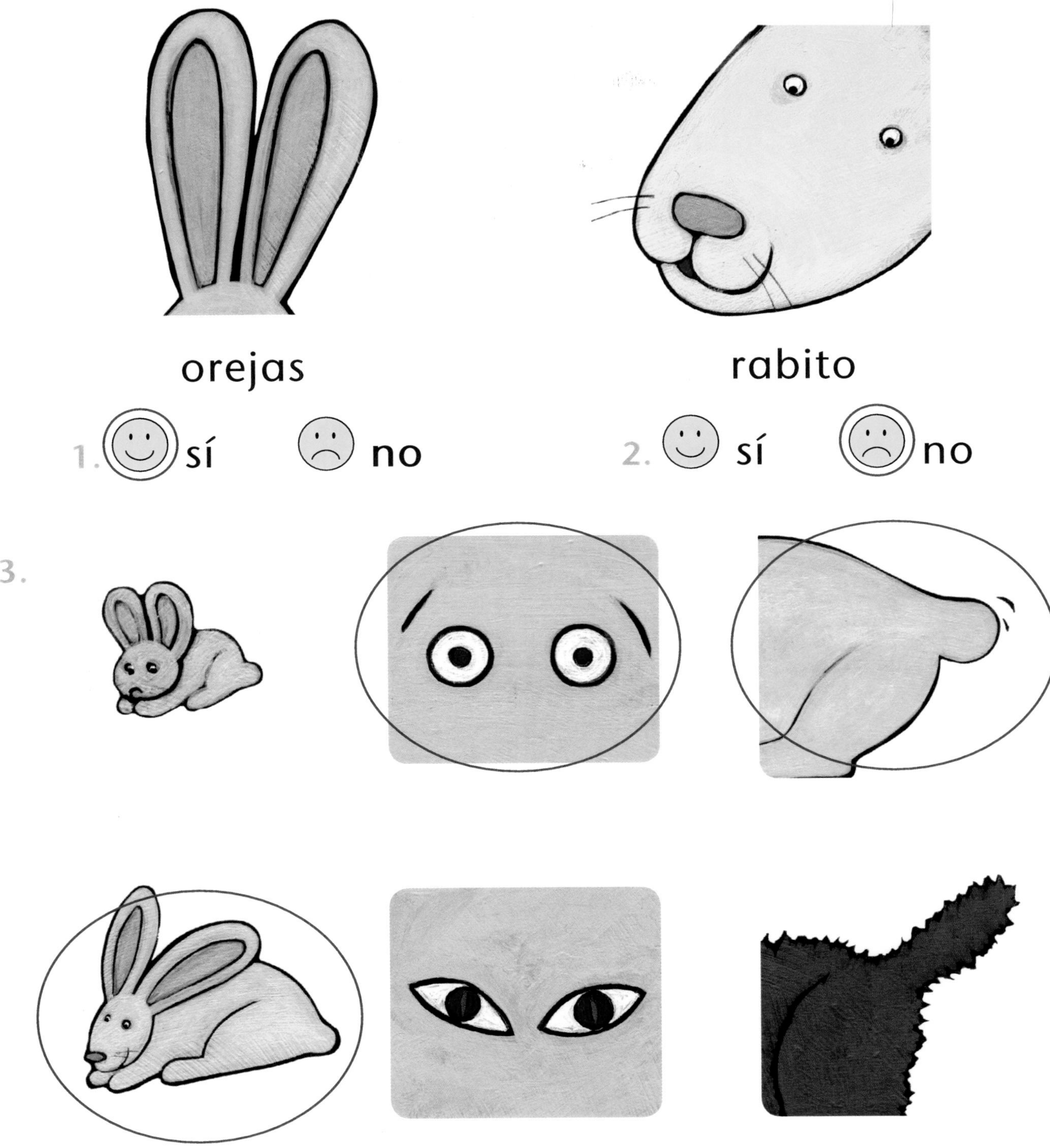

Así se dice

For items 1–4, point to the pictures as you say the words *ojos*, *orejas*, *oveja*, and *oso*. Clarify the meaning of all words. Have students repeat after you. Then show students how to spell the letter *O o*. For items 5 and 6, have students read the words aloud with you as they circle the correct answer on the answer sheet.

O o

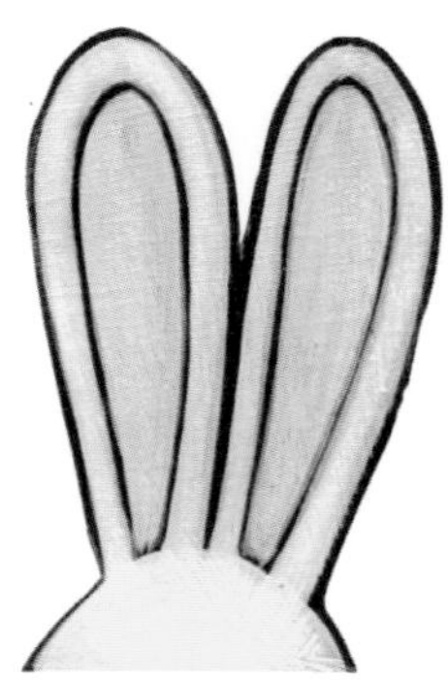

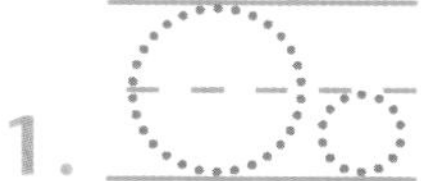

1. O o

2. O o

3. O o

4. O o

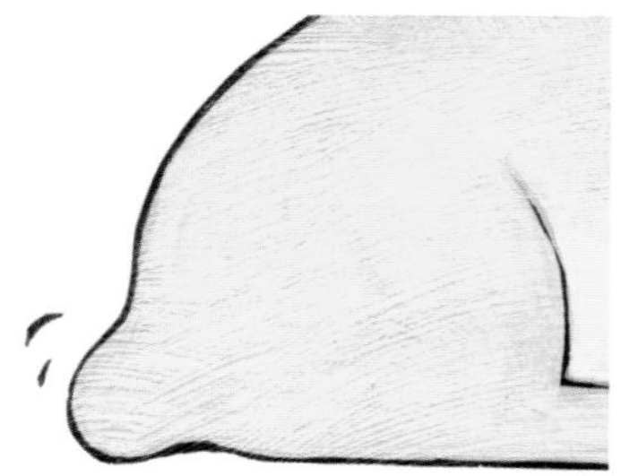

5. ojos  orejas

6. rabito hociquito

Así se escribe

Explain that words can name one or more than one thing, and that sometimes we add an s at the end of the word when we want to name more than one thing. For items 1–4, read each word aloud emphasizing the ending. Ask students whether each word expresses one or more than one, and have them circle the correct picture.

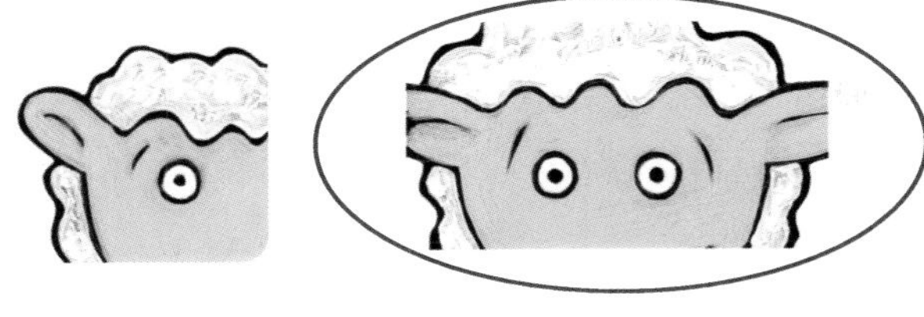

1. ojos

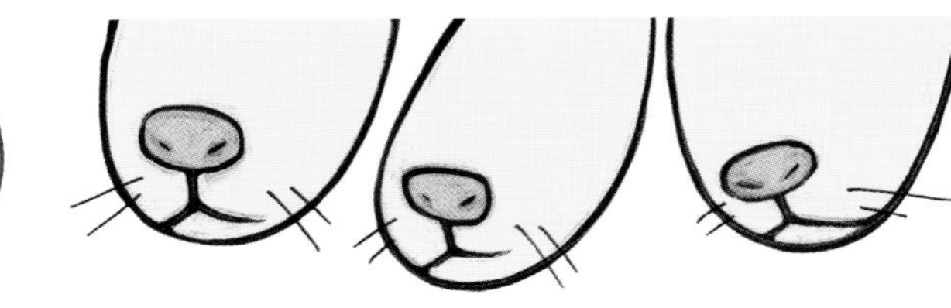

2. hocico

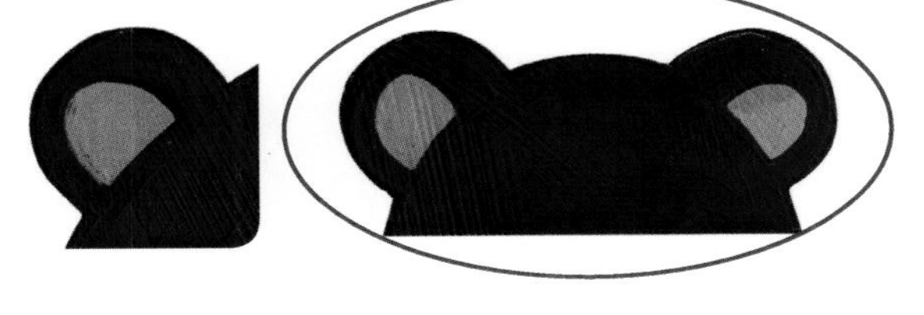

3. orejas

4. rabo

A escribir

Review story vocabulary. Read the question and the sentence and have students complete it by writing the missing letters. Then ask students to draw their favorite animal and two of its body parts. Encourage them to share their work.

- ¿Qué tiene?

El O so tiene O jos y O rejas.

tiene y .

Answers will vary.

Briefly discuss the five senses. Explain that today they will focus on three of them and parts of the face. Help students mention things they can see, smell, or taste. Ask: *¿Qué ven con sus ojos?* What do you see with your eyes? *¿Qué huelen con su nariz?* What do you smell with your nose? *¿Qué comen con su boca?* What do you taste with your mouth? Have students view the illustrations and help them "read" them. Ask students to describe what the boy is doing in each illustration. Have students point to the title as you read it aloud. Invite students to read along with you. Ask students what they think the story might be about based on the title and the illustrations.

Tengo dos ojos.

Veo una uva con mis ojos.

Read the text aloud. Remind students that sentences are made up of groups of words. Read the text again and have students clap at the end of every sentence. Encourage them to chorally read along with you, pointing to each body part as it is read. Emphasize the u sound in words that begin with that letter.

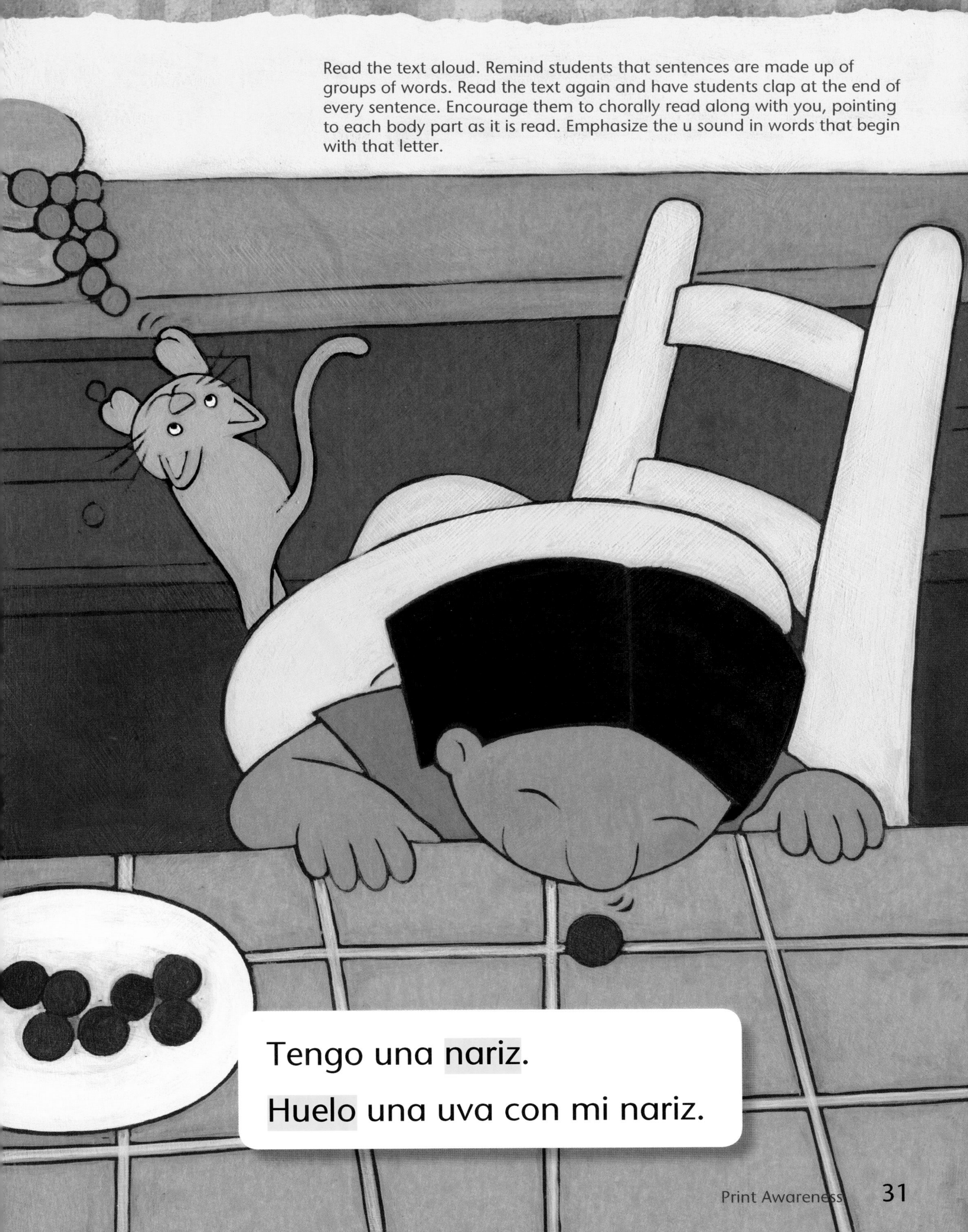

Tengo una nariz.

Huelo una uva con mi nariz.

Discuss the order of events in the story. Read the story again and have students act out what happens first, next, and last by using the time-order words *primero*, *después*, and *por último*. Review vocabulary and encourage students to retell the events using the words.

Tengo una boca.

Como una uva con mi boca. ¡Um!

Comprendo lo que leí

Discuss the selection and help students complete the activities on the answer sheets. For items 1–2, have students circle the correct answer. For item 3, have students number the pictures to show the order of events in the story.

como

1.  sí no

huelo

2.  sí no

3.

Así se dice

For items 1–4, point to the pictures as you say the words *uva, uno, uña,* and *uniforme.* Clarify the meaning of all words. Have students repeat after you. Then show students how to spell the letter *U u.* For items 5–6, have students read the words aloud with you as they circle the correct answer on the answer sheet.

U u

1. U u

2. U u

3. U u

4. U u

5. boca nariz

6. como veo

Así se escribe

Explain that descriptive words tell us about things, people, animals, and places. Explain that color words are descriptive words because they tell us the color of something. For items 1–3, have students complete the sentence by tracing the missing letter. Then help them identify each descriptive word. Have them color the pictures on the answer sheet purple and blue so they match the illustrations in the book.

1. Yo como ___vas moradas.

2. Yo tengo ojos az___les.

A escribir

Review story vocabulary and how to spell *o* and *u*. Read the question and the first sentence, and have students complete it by writing the missing letters. Then read the sentence starter and have them look around and complete the sentence by drawing something that they see.

- ¿Qué vemos?

Ulises ve U na U va con sus O jos.

Answers will vary.

Discuss different modes of transportation such as *barco, avión* and *carro* and where they can use them. Ask: *¿Cómo viajan por el agua?* How do you travel by water? *¿Cómo viajan por el aire?* How do you travel by air? *¿Cómo viajan por tierra?* How do you travel by land? Have students view the illustrations and help them "read them". Ask students to describe the place depicted. Mention that it is lake Puelo in Argentina. Elicit that the little boat is trying to sail through the lake but it can't. Conduct a picture walk and have students discuss what might happen in the story/song based on the illustrations.

El barquito

Tradicional

Había una vez un barco pequeñito que no podía navegar.

Read the text aloud several times and have students repeat after you. Then play the audio of the song and have students repeat the lines as they sing along. Encourage students to count with their fingers as they sing the number of weeks the boat has been stranded. Emphasize the *p* sound.

Pasaron una, dos, tres, cuatro, cinco, seis, siete semanas.

Have students discuss the setting of the story. Sing the song again and have students act out what happens to the little boat. Ask what clues in the illustrations help understand what happens to the little boat. Elicit ways, such as visiting the library or using the Internet, students could find more information about means of transportation and about lake Puelo in Argentina.

Y el barquito no podía navegar.

Comprendo lo que leí

Discuss the selection and help students complete the activities on the answer sheets. For items 1–2, have students circle the correct answer. For item 3, have students complete the sentence by tracing the letter *P*. Then ask them to show the setting of the story by drawing the place where the boat is located after seven weeks.

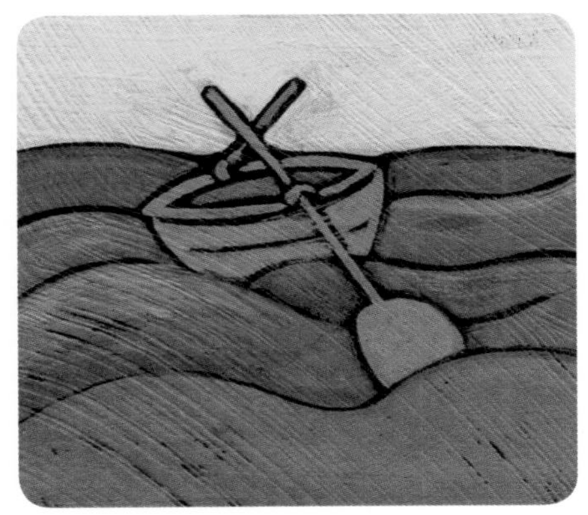

pequeñito

1.  sí  no

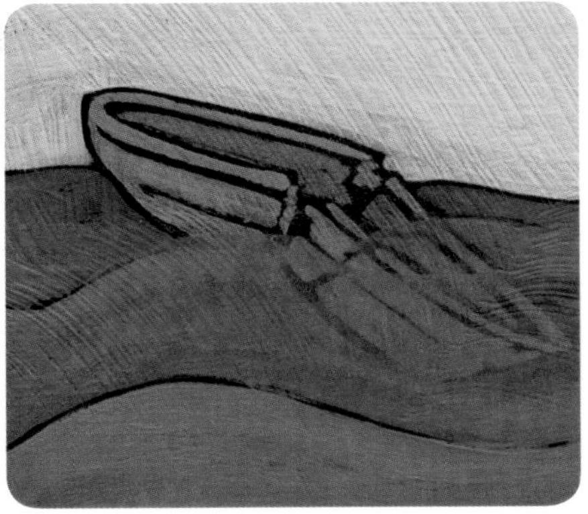

navegar

2.  sí  no

3. Pasaron siete semanas.

Students draw a winter scene, which shows the little boat after seven weeks.

Así se dice

For item 1, point to the picture and say the word *papá*. Clarify its meaning and show students how to spell the letter *P p*. For items 2–6, point to the pictures as you say the words *pajarito*, *perro*, *piña*, *pollito*, and *puma*. Clarify the meaning of all words. Have students repeat after you. Then show students how to spell the syllables *pa*, *pe*, *pi*, *po*, and *pu*.

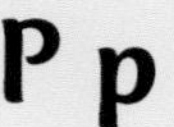

1. P p

2. pa jarito

3. pe rro

4. pi ña

5. po llito

6. pu ma

Así se escribe

Remind students that descriptive words tell us what something looks like. Explain that *grande* means big. For items 1–3, read each word aloud and have students circle the word that best describes each picture.

1. grande pequeño

2. grande pequeño

3. grande pequeño

A escribir

Review story vocabulary and the syllables *pa* and *pe*. Read the question and the first sentence. Have students complete it by writing the missing syllables. Then read the sentence starter and have them complete the sentence by drawing the mode of transportation they use more frequently.

- ¿Cómo viajamos?

El pajarito y el perro viajan en barco.

Yo viajo en ______.

Answers will vary.

Discuss students' personal interests and favorite professions. Ask: *¿Qué les gusta hacer?* What do you like to do? *¿Qué quieren ser?* What do you want to be? *¿Dónde quieren trabajar?* Where do you want to work? Read the title and the author's name and have students read along. Then have students view the pictures and help them "read" them. Ask them to describe the people depicted.

¿Qué quieres ser?

Amy White
adaptación

¡Mira! A este niño le gusta la escuela. Quiere ser maestro.

Review vowel sounds with students. Then read the text aloud several times and have students chorally read along. Point to the word *maestro*. Emphasize the *m* sound as you read it. Read the selection again and have students stand up every time they hear the *m* sound.

¡Mira! A esta niña le gustan los animales.

Quiere ser veterinaria.

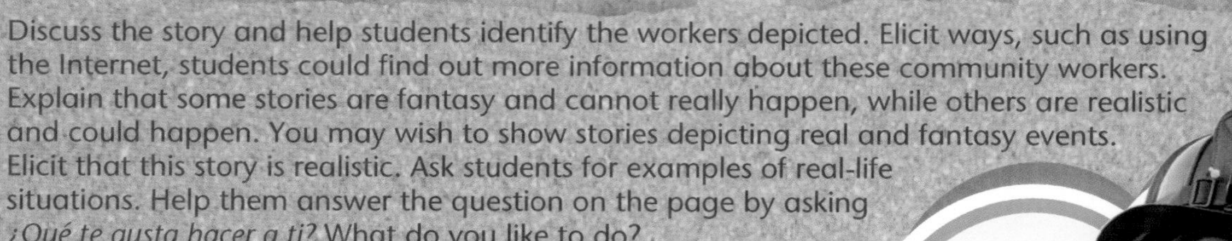

Discuss the story and help students identify the workers depicted. Elicit ways, such as using the Internet, students could find out more information about these community workers. Explain that some stories are fantasy and cannot really happen, while others are realistic and could happen. You may wish to show stories depicting real and fantasy events. Elicit that this story is realistic. Ask students for examples of real-life situations. Help them answer the question on the page by asking *¿Qué te gusta hacer a ti?* What do you like to do?

bombera

músico

mecánico

doctora

¿Qué quieres ser tú?

Comprendo lo que leí

Discuss the selection and help students complete the activities on the answer sheets. For items 1–2, have students circle the correct answer. For item 3, have students mark an X next to the picture that shows a real-life situation.

veterinario

1. sí no

maestra

2. sí no

3.

not marked

X

Así se dice

For item 1, point to the picture and say the word *mamá*. Clarify its meaning and show students how to spell the letter *M m*. For items 2–6, point to the pictures as you say the words *maestra*, *mecánico*, *minero*, *modista*, and *muñeca*. Clarify the meaning of all words. Have students repeat after you. Then show them how to spell the syllables *ma*, *me*, *mi*, *mo*, and *mu*.

M m

1. Mm

2. maestra

3. mecánico

4. minero

5. modista

6. muñeca

Así se escribe

Remind students that we use naming words for things, people, animals, and places. Read each sentence and have students trace the letters that complete each naming word. Have students sound out the letters as they trace them.

1. El ma estro trabaja en una e scuela. ma, e

2. El a rtista trabaja en un mu seo. a, mu

A escribir

Review story vocabulary. Read the question and the sentence and have students complete it by writing the missing letters. Then read the sentence starter and have them complete the sentence by drawing the profession they would like to have as adults. Encourage students to share their work.

- ¿Qué quieres ser?

El niño quiere ser ma estro.

Yo quiero ser .

Answers will vary.

Discuss holidays and traditions with students. Ask: *¿Cuál es su feriado favorito?* What's your favorite holiday? *¿Cómo lo celebran?* How do you celebrate it? *¿Qué decoraciones usan?* What kinds of decorations do you use? Have students point to the title and the author of the story as you read this information aloud. Then have them view the illustrations and help them "read" them. Ask students to describe what is going on in the illustrations. Elicit that the girl is decorating a tree to celebrate the holidays in her small village in Colombia.

Arbolito de mi aldea

Mario Castro

Arbolito de mi aldea,
eres mi amigo de verdad.

Read the text aloud several times and have students chorally repeat after you. Emphasize the *n* sound. Then play the audio of the song and have students track print as they sing along. Once students learn the song, encourage them to move around in a circle as they sing along.

Gente alegre te rodea.

No te importa nuestra edad.

Explain that sometimes authors write to teach us something, and sometimes to entertain us. Elicit that here the author's purpose is to entertain. Discuss other ways to learn more about holidays in Colombia.

¡Tus luces dicen que todos somos niños en Navidad!

Comprendo lo que leí

Discuss the selection and help students complete the activities on the answer sheets. For items 1–2, have students circle the correct answer. For item 3, have students complete the picture by drawing themselves singing the song and moving around in a circle. Explain that this shows the author's purpose for writing this song: to entertain.

arbolito

1.  sí  no

alegre

2.  sí  no

3. La canción es alegre.

Answers will vary.

Así se dice

For item 1, point to the picture and say the word *Navidad*. Clarify its meaning and show students how to spell the letter *N n*. For items 2–6, point to the images as you say the words *naranja, nene, niña, noche,* and *nube*. Clarify the meaning of all words. Have students repeat after you. Then show them how to spell the syllables *na, ne, ni, no,* and *nu*.

N n

1. Nn

2. na ranja

3. ne ne

4. ni ña

5. no che

6. nu be

Así se escribe

Remind students that words can name one or more than one thing, and that we often add an *s* at the end of a word when we want to name more than one thing. For items 1–3, read each word aloud emphasizing the ending and have students complete it by tracing the missing letter. Then ask students whether each word expresses one or more than one, and have them circle the correct image.

1. na ranjas

2. ni ño

3. nu bes

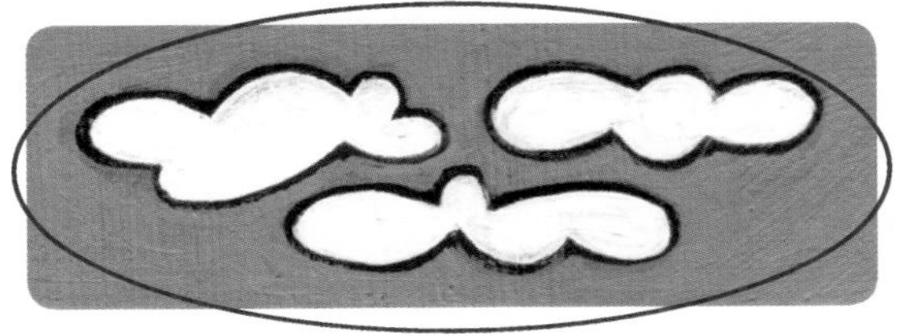

A escribir

Review story vocabulary. Read the question and the sentence and have students complete it by writing the missing letters. Then read the sentence starter and have students complete the sentence by drawing a holiday they celebrate. Encourage students to add details to their drawing that show how they celebrate. Have students share their drawings.

- ¿Qué celebramos?

Los **ni** ños celebran la **Na** vidad.

Yo celebro ______ .

Answers will vary.

Discuss family relations. Ask: *¿Tienen hermanos o hermanas?* Do you have brothers or sisters? *¿Piensan que es bueno tener hermanos y hermanas?* Do you think it's good to have brothers and sisters? *¿Qué les gusta jugar con sus familiares?* What games do you like to play with your family members?

Have students point to the title and the author of the story. Then read this information aloud. Mention that the author of this story is also the illustrator. Discuss that the illustrator draws the pictures in a story. Then have them view the illustrations and help them "read"them. Ask students to describe the characters in the illustrations. Elicit that the girls are sisters.

Por si no te lo he dicho

María Fernanda Heredia
adaptación

¿Te he dicho que tienes ojos de sapo?

Read the text aloud several times and have students read along with you. Encourage them to track print as they read along. Emphasize the *s* sound, and remind students that the *h* is silent. Explain that letter sounds can form combined sounds. Give some examples of syllables from the reading, such as *sa-po, o-cho , bi-go-te, her-ma-na*. Explain that these combined sounds are called syllables and are like "building blocks" used to form words. Elicit from volunteers some words with two or three syllables.

¿Te he dicho que cuando cumplas ocho te saldrá bigote?

Discuss the characters and their relationship. Explain that we can use clues from the reading and what we already know to figure out something that is not explained in the story. Encourage students to find clues in the story to help them describe the characters.

Me queda una cosa por decirte,
y esta sí es verdad...
Me gusta mucho que seas mi hermana.

Comprendo lo que leí

Discuss the selection and help students complete the activities on the answer sheets. For items 1–2, have students circle the correct answer. For item 3, have them mark an X on the pictures that show things they can guess from the story.

hermana

1. **(sí)** no

verdad

2. sí **(no)**

3.

not marked

Así se dice

For item 1, point to the picture and say the word *sapo*. Show students how to spell the letter *S s*. For items 2–6, point to the pictures as you say the words. Have students repeat after you. Then show them how to spell the syllables *sa, se, si, so,* and *su*. For item 7, have students match each word with the correct illustration on the answer sheet.

Así se escribe

Explain that we capitalize the first letter in a sentence. Have students look for examples of capitalized words in the story. For items 1–3, read the sentence and ask students to trace the syllable that completes each word. You may "write" the letters on the floor using masking tape and have students walk on the letters.

1. So mos hermanas.

2. No tenemos ojos de sa po.

3. Sa limos a jugar.

A escribir

Review story vocabulary and the syllable *so*. Read the question and the sentences and have students write the missing syllables. Then have students complete the second sentence by drawing their family.

- ¿Cómo es tu familia?

En mi familia **SO** mos dos hermanas, papá y mamá.

En mi familia **SO** mos

.

Answers will vary.

Discuss what different types of dwellings look like. Then discuss some chores children do at home, such as picking up their toys. Ask: *¿Cómo es su casa?* What does your house look like? *¿Cómo ayudan en su casa?* What chores do you do at home?

Read the title and explain that the story is a tongue twister, or *trabalenguas*, about a young woman who is putting a roof on her shack. Then have students view the illustrations and help them "read" them. Ask students to describe María Chucena's home. Mention that her home is in a town close to Machu Picchu in Perú.

María Chucena

Tradicional

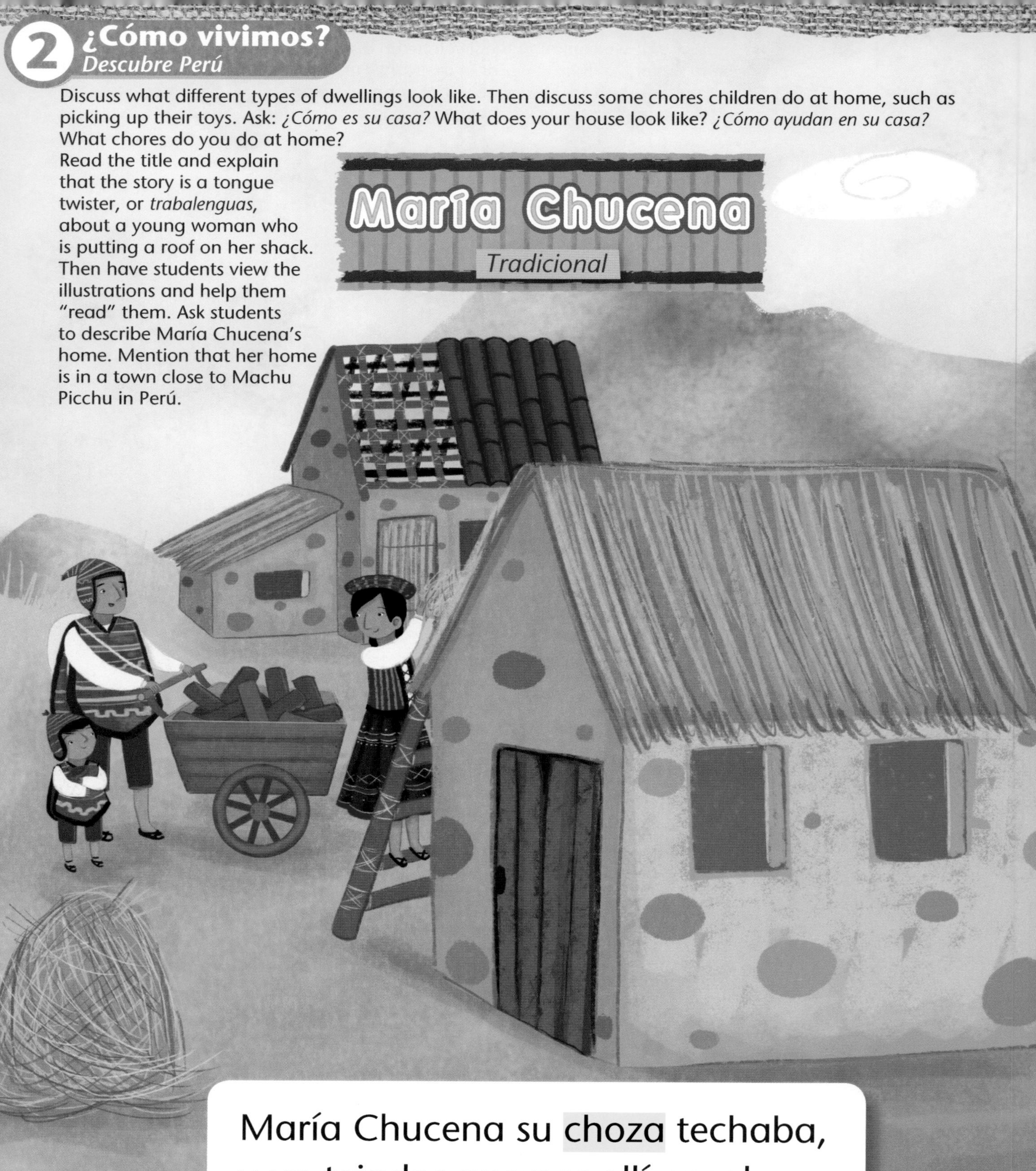

María Chucena su choza techaba,
y un tejador que por allí pasaba
le dijo:

Read the text aloud several times and have students read along with you, tracking print. Emphasize the *ch* sound by having students make the sound of a choo choo train. Remind them that letter sounds can form combined sounds called syllables. Provide examples of syllables from the reading, such as *cho-za*, *Chu-ce -na*, and *te-cho*. Point to the corresponding images as you say each word.

—María Chucena,
¿tú techas tu choza o techas la ajena?

Discuss new vocabulary. Then tell students that when they tell how two things are alike, they are comparing. Ask students to compare María Chucena's home to their own. Model an example using words like *puerta, ventana, techo, campo, ciudad, grande, pequeña*, etc.

Y ella le dijo:
—Yo techo mi choza.
No techo la ajena.
Yo techo la choza de María Chucena.

Comprendo lo que leí

Discuss the selection and help students complete the activities on the answer sheets. For items 1–2, have students circle the correct answer. For item 3, read the first caption and have students draw María Chucena's house. Then read the second caption and have students draw their house. Finally, have them compare both homes.

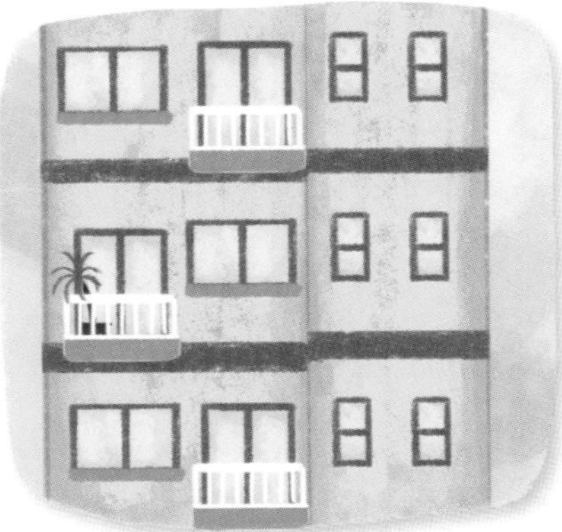

choza

1. sí  no

techas

2. sí no

3. La choza de María Chucena Students should draw María Chucena's home.

Mi casa Answers will vary.

Así se dice

For item 1, point to the girl and say her last name, *Chucena*. Show students how to spell *Ch ch*. For items 2–6, point to the pictures as you say the words. Have students repeat after you. Then show them how to spell *cha*, *che*, *chi*, *cho*, and *chu*. For items 7–8, have students read the words aloud as they circle the correct answer on the answer sheet.

Ch ch

1. Ch ch

2. chaleco

3. chef

4. chico

5. choza

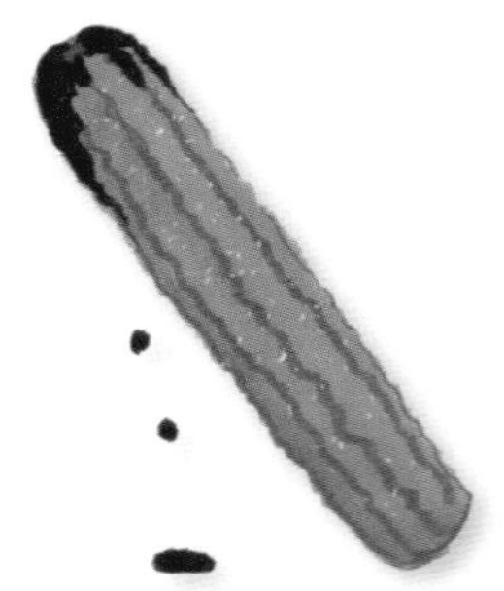

6. churro

7. (mi choza) la ajena

8. mi choza  (la ajena)

Así se escribe

Review that naming words are words that name things, people, animals, and places. For items 1–2, read the sentence and have students trace the syllable that completes each naming word.

1. María vive en una cho za y lleva puesto un cha leco.

2. El chi co lleva puesto un pon cho.

A escribir

Review story vocabulary and the syllables *cha*, *cho*, and *chu*. Read the question and the sentences and have students write the missing syllables. Then have students complete the second sentence by drawing a chore they do at home. Encourage them to share their work.

- ¿Cómo ayudamos en casa?

María Chu cena te cha su cho za.

Yo . Answers will vary.

3 Vamos a aprender
Descubre República Dominicana

Discuss different activities children can do at school. Ask: *¿Qué actividades hacen en la escuela?* What activities do you do at school? *¿Qué actividades son divertidas?* Which activities are fun? *¿Qué actividades no son divertidas?* Which activities are not fun?

Read the title and the author's name. Then have students view the illustrations and help them "read" them. Ask students to describe where the children are and what activities they are doing.

Este es el salón de clase de kindergarten.
¡Hay muchas cosas que hacer en clase!

Read the text aloud several times and have students read along with you, tracking print. Emphasize the *i* sound. Then have students name each activity as they point to the corresponding image. Next, say *Yo leo* y *escribo. Yo dibujo y pinto.* Ask students to repeat after you as they mimic these activities.

En clase, lees y escribes.
En clase, dibujas y pintas.

Discuss new vocabulary. Then tell students that the most important thing the author says in a story or a paragraph is called the main idea, and that it can usually be found at the beginning of the text. Reread the text and help students identify the main idea, *hay muchas cosas que hacer en la clase de kindergarten,* in the selection. Have them point to the main idea or track print as you reread it.

En clase, cantas y tocas música.
En clase, aprendes los números.
¡El salón de clase está lleno de cosas divertidas!

Comprendo lo que leí

Discuss the selection and help students complete the activities on the answer sheets. For items 1–2, have students circle the correct answer. For item 3, have them mark an X on the image that shows the main idea of the reading.

tocas música

1. (sí) no

dibujas

2. sí (no)

3.

☐

not marked

☒

Así se dice

For item 1, point to the picture and say the word *lee*. Show students how to spell the letter *L l*. For items 2–6, point to the images as you say the words. Have students repeat after you. Then show them how to spell the syllables *la*, *le*, *li*, *lo*, and *lu*. For items 7 and 8, have students read the words aloud with you as they circle the correct answer on the answer sheet.

L l

1. Ll

2. lazo

3. leche

4. libro

5. loro

6. luna

7. canta (escribe)

8. lee (pinta)

Así se escribe

Explain that there are words that express an action, such as *leer*, *dibujar* and *cantar*. Elicit other action words, such as *comer*, *aprender*, etc. For items 1–3, read each word and have students trace the missing syllables. Then have students circle the words that express an action on the answer sheet.

1. le en

2. la va

3. lo ro

4. li bro

A escribir

Review story vocabulary and the syllables *le* and *li*. Read the question and the sentence, and have students write in the missing syllables. Then have students complete the second sentence by drawing two things they do in their kindergarten classroom. Encourage students to label their drawings.

- ¿Qué hacemos en el salón de clase?

Los niños le en un li bro.

Yo . Answers will vary.

Discuss popular pets and help students describe them. Ask: *¿Qué es una mascota?* What is a pet? *¿Qué mascotas tienen?* Which pets do you have? *¿Cómo son sus mascotas?* What do your pets look like? Read the title of the song. Then have students view the illustrations and help them "read" them. Help students describe the animals depicted and what activities they are doing. Elicit that Pirulín and Pirulón are the names of the two cats.

Tradicional

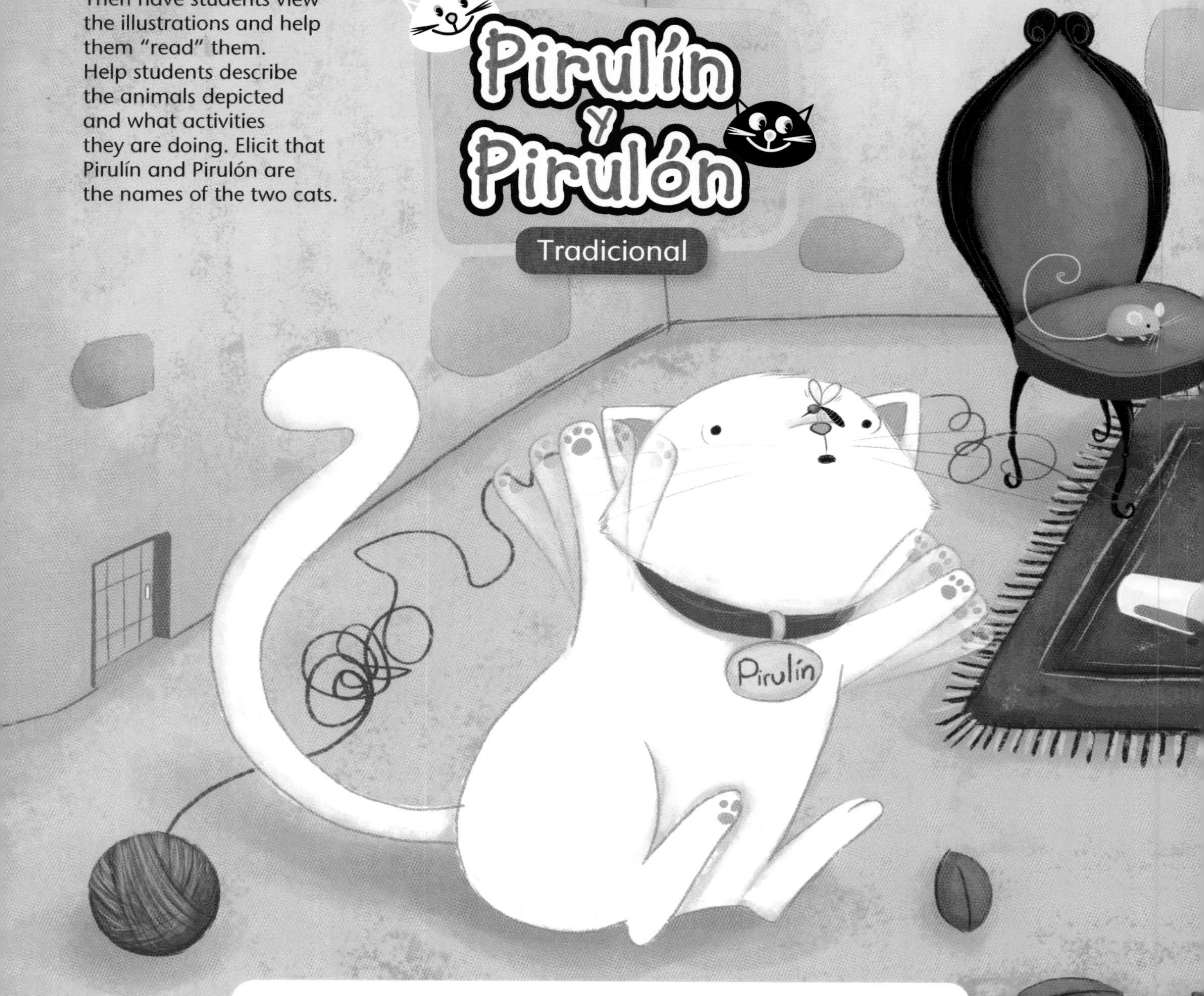

Había dos gatitos
junto al fuego del salón:
el blanco Pirulín y el negro Pirulón.
¡Pirulín, Pirulón, Pirulín, Pirulón!

Read the text aloud several times and have students read along with you, tracking print. Emphasize the initial *r* sound in *rata* and *ratón*. Have students touch their throats to feel the vibrations as they pronounce the *r* sound. Next, remind students that words that end with the same sound are called rhyming words. Help students find the rhyming words in this song. Then play the audio of the song and have students repeat the lines as they sing along.

Cazaban los mosquitos,
ni una rata ni un ratón:
el blanco Pirulín y el negro Pirulón.
¡Pirulín, Pirulón, Pirulín, Pirulón!

Discuss new vocabulary. Then help students identify the main characters in the song/story (Pirulín and Pirulón) and the secondary characters (the mosquitoes, the rat, the mouse, and mom). Have students describe the cats' traits based on the song and the illustrations.

Su mamá los bañaba
con cepillo y con jabón:
el blanco Pirulín y el negro Pirulón.
¡Pirulín, Pirulón, Pirulín, Pirulón!

Comprendo lo que leí

Help students complete the activities on the answer sheets. For items 1–2, have students circle the correct answer. For item 3, have students draw the main characters in the story. Be sure they color each cat appropriately and that they include something that shows the cats' traits such as happy faces, etc. Encourage students to label the main characters' names.

el gato negro

1. sí  no

los mosquitos

2. sí no

3.

Students should draw Pirulín (white cat) and Pirulón (black cat).

Así se dice

For item 1, point to the picture and say the word *ratón*. Show students how to spell the letter *R r*. For items 2–6, point to the images as you say the words. Have students repeat after you. Then show them how to spell the syllables *ra, re, ri, ro,* and *ru*. For items 7–8, have students read the words aloud with you as they circle the correct answer on the answer sheet.

R r

1. R r

2. ra ta

3. re loj

4. ri sa

5. ro jo

6. ru bia

7. jabón negro

8. blanco gatitos

Así se escribe

Remind students that words can name one or more than one thing and that sometimes we add an *s* at the end of the word when we want to name more than one thing. For items 1–4, read each word aloud emphasizing the ending. Ask students whether each word expresses one or more than one, and have them circle the correct picture.

1. mosquito

2. ratones

3. gatito

4. ratas

A escribir

Review story vocabulary and the syllable *ra*. Read the question and the sentence and have students write in the missing syllables. Then have students complete the second sentence by drawing their favorite pet. Encourage them to draw traits of their favorite pet.

- ¿Cómo son las mascotas?

Pirulón es negro. No caza ni **ra**tones ni **ra**tas.

Mi mascota es ______.

Answers will vary.

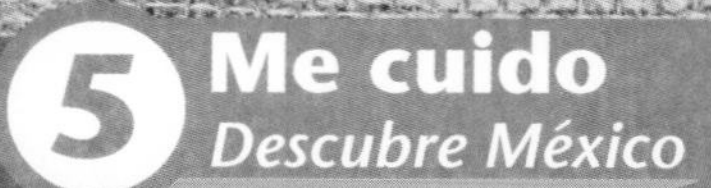

5 Me cuido
Descubre México

Discuss healthy habits, such as washing our hands, brushing our teeth, eating healthy food, and exercising. Ask: *¿Qué hacen para estar saludables?* What do you do to stay healthy? *¿Por qué necesitamos hacer ejercicio?* Why do we need to exercise?

Read the title of the song and the names of the authors. Then have students view the illustrations and help them "read" them. Help students describe what activities the children are doing. Elicit that they are trying to stay healthy.

Cuerpos saludables

Patricia E. Acosta y Mario Castro

Vamos a cepillarnos.
Los dientes hay que lavar.
Vamos a peinarnos
y luego a desayunar.

Read the text aloud several times and have students read along with you, tracking print. Emphasize the *y* sound in *hay* and *desayunar*. Then play the audio of the song and have students repeat the lines as they sing along. Encourage them to dance like the children in the illustrations.

Nos gusta estar activos.
Los cuerpos hay que mover.
Para estar saludables
esto nos gusta hacer:

Discuss new vocabulary. Then remind students that authors have different reasons for writing a song or a story, such as entertaining, giving information, explaining something, or convincing others to do something. Elicit that the authors' main purpose is to convince others to have healthy habits. Ask students about different ways they could learn more about healthy habits, such as reading a book, asking teachers, or having an adult help them search the Internet.

¡Sacudir las manos!
¡Levantar los pies!
¡Luego dar la media vuelta
una y otra vez!

Comprendo lo que leí

Discuss the selection and help students complete the activities on the answer sheets. For items 1–2, have students circle the correct answer. For item 3, have students complete the illustration by drawing the children dancing and then drawing themselves performing a healthy activity. Explain that this shows the authors' purpose for writing this song: to convince others to have healthy habits.

desayunar

1. sí  no

peinar

2. sí no

3.

Answers will vary.

Así se dice

For item 1, point to the image and say the word *yate*. Guide students in spelling *Y y*. For items 2–6, point to the images as students repeat after you. Then show them how to spell *ya, ye, yi, yo,* and *yu*. For item 7, have students match the word with the correct illustration on the answer sheet. Then have them circle the words for parts of the body.

Y y

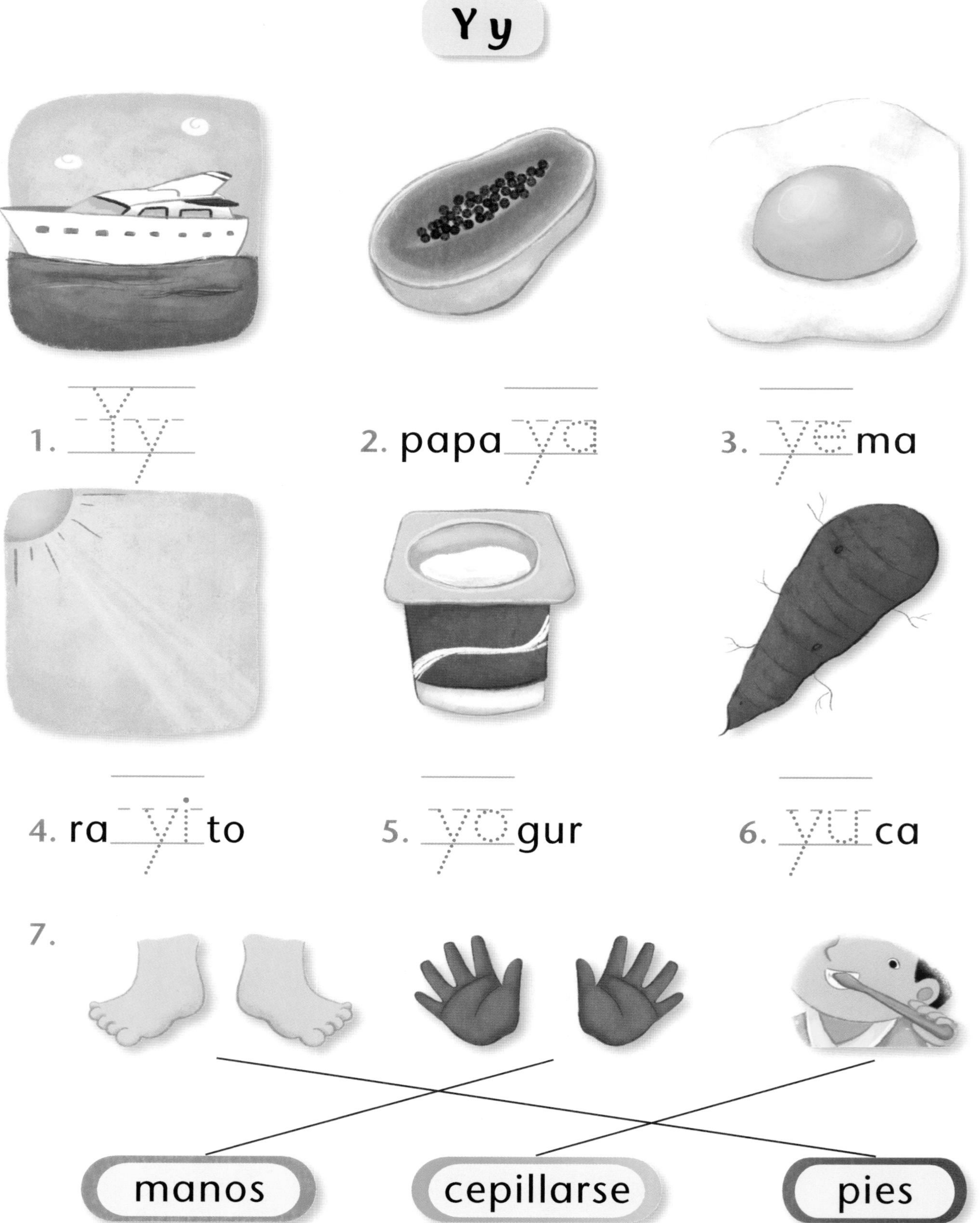

Así se escribe

Explain that descriptive words, or adjectives, tell us about things, people, animals, and places. For items 1–3, read the sentences and have students complete each word by tracing the missing syllable. Then read each sentence again and the two descriptive words that follow. Have students circle the word that best describes the noun in each sentence.

1. El yo gur es... (suave) duro.
2. El yа te es... pequeño (grande).
3. La ye ma es... (amarilla) verde.

A escribir

Review the syllables *yo* and *yu*. Discuss healthy habits. Read the question and the sentence and have students write the missing syllables. Then have them complete the second sentence by drawing two things they do to stay healthy. Point to the letter *y* and elicit that it's also a word that means "and".

- ¿Qué hacemos para estar saludables?

El niño desa yu na yo gur.

Yo  y .

Answers will vary.

Discuss the seasons and different activities people can do in each season. Ask: *¿Cuáles son las estaciones del año?* What are the seasons of the year? *¿Qué actividades podemos hacer durante cada estación?* What activities can we do during each season?

Read the title of the text. Then have students view the images and help them "read" them. Help students describe what season is shown and what activities the children are doing in each image.

Las estaciones

Amy White
Adaptación

¿Cuál de las estaciones te gusta más?
¿Te gusta la primavera?
En la primavera puedes ver flores
de todos los colores.

Read the text aloud several times and have students read along with you, tracking print. Emphasize the *v* sound in *primavera, ver, verano, invierno* and *nieve*. Choose two-syllable words from the story, such as *flores, parque* and *hojas*, and ask students to orally separate them into syllables. Have them clap as they say each syllable.

¿Te gusta el verano?
En el verano puedes nadar todo el día.
También puedes ir al parque y comer afuera.

Discuss new vocabulary. Then remind students that authors have different reasons for writing a text. Elicit that this author's main purpose is to give information about the seasons. Ask students about different media, such as books, magazines, and the Internet, where they could find more illustrations and facts about the different seasons.

¿Te gusta el otoño?
En el otoño puedes saltar en las hojas.
¿Te gusta el invierno?
En el invierno puedes jugar en la nieve.

Comprendo lo que leí

Discuss the selection and help students complete the activities on the answer sheets. For items 1–2, have students circle the correct answer. For item 3, review the author's purpose (to give information about the seasons). Then read the caption and have students complete it by tracing the missing syllable. Finally, have students draw a picture showing what the author wanted them to learn about spring.

otoño

1. (sí) no

verano

2. sí (no)

3. La prima ve ra

Answers will vary.

Así se dice

For item 1, point to the picture and say the word *verde*. Show students how to spell the letter *V v*. For items 2–6, point to the images as you say the words. Have students repeat after you. Then show them how to spell *va, ve, vi, vo*, and *vu*. For item 7, read the words aloud and have students match each season with the correct word and illustration.

1. V v
2. va so
3. ve rano
4. vi ento
5. pa vo
6. vu ela
7.

primavera

otoño

invierno

Así se escribe

Explain that sometimes we create new words when we change syllables. For items 1–3, guide students in orally separating the words into syllables. Identify the syllable being changed and read the new word. Have students trace the missing syllable to complete the new word.

1. 

pi – so

va – so

piso

va so

2. 

co – la

ve – la

cola

ve la

3. 

pa – pel

pa – vo

papel

pa vo

A escribir

Review story vocabulary and the syllable *ve*. Read the question and the sentence and have students write the missing syllable. Then have students complete the sentence by drawing something they do in the summer. Encourage them to share their work and to compare and contrast what they and their classmates do in the summer.

- ¿Qué hacemos en el verano?

En el ve rano, yo .

Answers will vary.

7 ¿Cómo funciona?
Descubre Panamá

Discuss the importance of workers and professionals in the community. Ask: *¿Por qué son todos los trabajadores importantes para la comunidad? ¿Cuáles son algunos?* Why are all community workers important? What are some of them? Encourage students to come up with Spanish or English words for doctors, teachers, police officers, firefighters, etc. Elicit they're important because they heal, save, help, teach, etc. Read the title and the author's name. Then have students view the images and help them "read" them. Help students identify all the workers depicted. Have them point to each worker as they identify them.

Lo que vamos a ser

Alma Flor Ada
fragmento

Todos nos preguntan
qué vamos a ser.

Read the text aloud several times and have students chorally read along with you, tracking text. Emphasize the *g* sound in the word *elegir*. Explain that when the *g* is next to an *e* or an *i*, it has a sound similar to the English *h*. Practice other words with the *ge* and *gi* sounds, such as *colegio*, *gigante*, and *gente*. Encourage students to "pant" as they make these sounds. Finally, have them look for pairs of rhyming words in the poem (escritora / pintora , encantos / tantos).

¿Capitán de un barco,
médica, escultora,
dentista, arquitecto,
escritor, pintora?

Discuss new vocabulary. Then explain to students that they can make inferences when they use clues from a reading and what they already know to figure out something. Read the poem again and help students make inferences by asking: *¿Por qué creen que es difícil elegir un oficio o profesión?* Why do you think it is difficult to choose a job or profession? Ask students about different media, such as television, advertisements, and signs, where they may have seen or heard about some professionals in their community.

Todos los oficios
tienen sus encantos.
Elegir no es fácil,
¡son tantos y tantos!

Comprendo lo que leí

Discuss the selection and help students complete the activities on the answer sheets. For items 1–2, have students circle the correct answer. For item 3, review students' answers to the question *¿Por qué creen que es difícil elegir un oficio o profesión?* Then have them mark an X on the image that shows something they can guess from the poem.

escultora

1. sí (no)

capitán

2. (sí) no

3.

not marked

X

Así se dice

For item 1, point to the picture and say the word *genio*. Show students how to spell the letter *G g*. For items 2–4, point to the images as you say the words. Have students repeat after you. Then show them how to spell *ge* and *gi*. For item 5, read the words aloud and have students match the word with the correct illustration on the answer sheet.

Así se escribe

For items 1–2, read the sentences and have students trace the letters that complete each naming word. Then contrast the use of capital and lowercase letters in each case. For item 3, remind students that sentences end with a punctuation mark, usually a period. Read the sentence and have students write the period at the end.

1. El ge neral se llama Ge rardo.

2. La gi mnasta se llama Gi sela.

3. No es fácil elegir un oficio ___

A escribir

Review story vocabulary and the syllable *ge*. Read the question and the sentence and have students write the missing syllable. Then read the sentence starter and have students complete the sentence by drawing the profession they would like to have as adults. Ask students to dictate the profession to you so that you can help them write the picture caption.

- ¿Qué vamos a ser?

Ella va a ser ge neral.

Yo voy a ser ______________________.

Answers will vary.

Discuss birthday celebrations. Ask: *¿Cómo celebran su cumpleaños?* How do you celebrate your birthday? *¿Qué decoraciones les gusta poner?* What decorations do you like? *¿Qué comidas les gusta comer?* What foods do you like to eat? *¿Qué juegos les gusta jugar?* What games do you like to play?

Read the title and the author's name. Then have students view the illustrations and predict what they think the story might be about. Help students identify the folktale characters depicted, *Ricitos de Oro* (Goldilocks), *Mamá Osa* (Mama Bear), *Papá Oso* (Papa Bear), and *Osito* (Baby Bear). Elicit that they are celebrating a birthday party.

Hoy es el cumpleaños de Ricitos de Oro.
Ella y sus amigos se divierten
en su fiesta de cumpleaños.
Primero todos juegan a romper la piñata.

Read the text aloud several times and have students chorally read along with you, tracking print. Emphasize the *f* sound in the words *fiesta*, *fuerte* and *feliz*. Choose two-syllable words from the story, such as *fiesta*, *juegan*, *alto*, *bajo*, *cantan*, *comen*, *fuerte*, and *suave*, and ask students to orally separate them into syllables. Have them clap as they say each syllable.

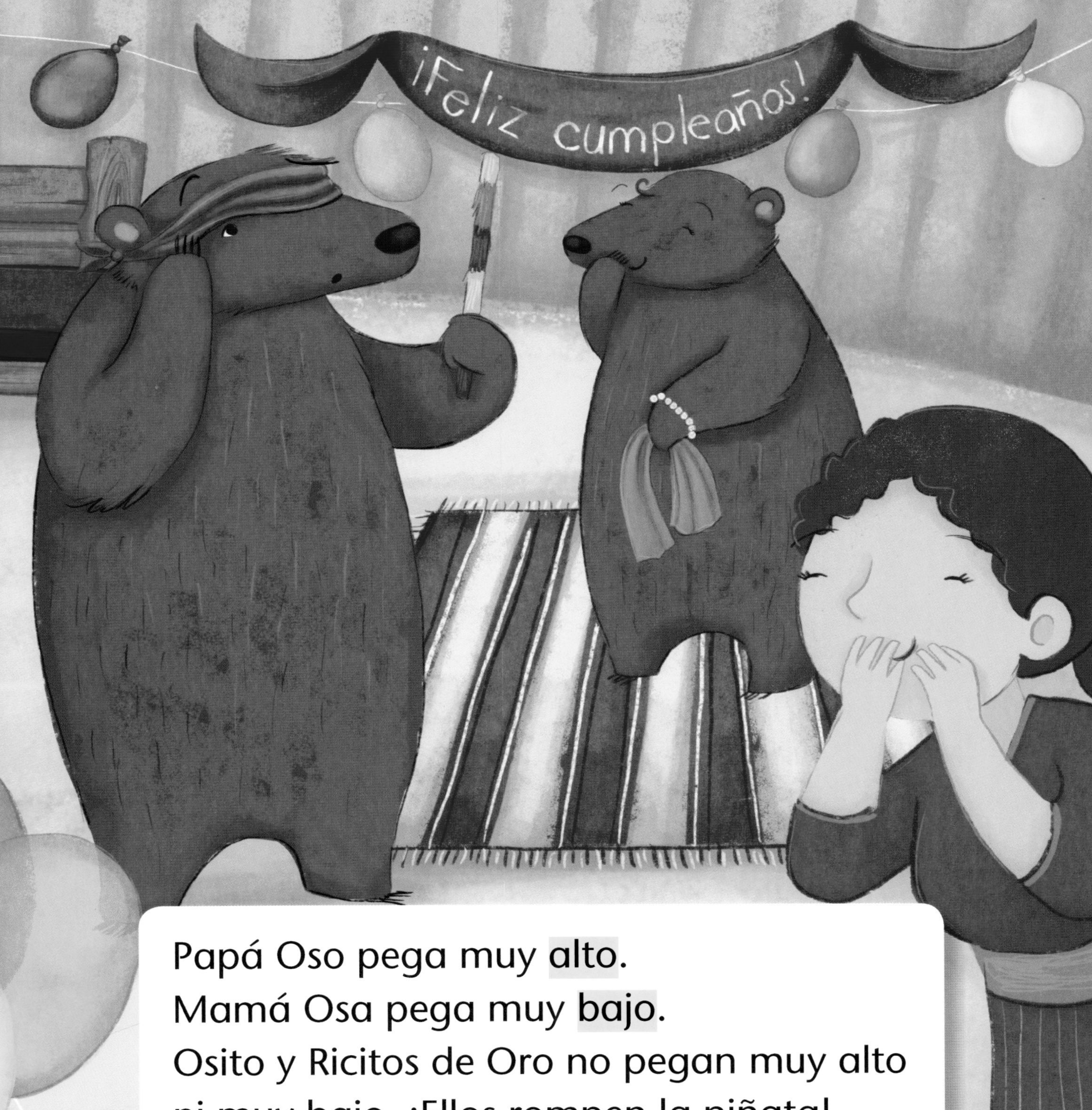

Papá Oso pega muy alto.
Mamá Osa pega muy bajo.
Osito y Ricitos de Oro no pegan muy alto ni muy bajo. ¡Ellos rompen la piñata!

Discuss new vocabulary. You may wish to have volunteers model each word and its meaning. Then remind students that words like *primero, después, luego, por último*, etc. can help them understand the order in which events take place in a story. Read the story again and help students identify words that signal order of events. Finally, have them retell the story using those words.

Luego todos cantan y comen pastel.
Papá Oso canta muy fuerte. Mamá Osa canta muy suave.
Osito y Ricitos de Oro no cantan muy fuerte ni muy suave. ¡Ellos cantan muy bien!
¡Feliz cumpleaños, Ricitos de Oro!

Comprendo lo que leí

Discuss the selection and help students complete the activities on the answer sheets. For items 1–2, have students circle the correct answer. For item 3, have students number the pictures to show the order of events in the story. Then have pairs of students take turns retelling the events.

cumpleaños

1. sí  no

cantan

2. sí no

3.

2

3

1

Así se dice

For item 1, point to the picture and say the word *flor*. Show students how to spell the letter *F f*. For items 2–6, point to the images as you say the words. Have students repeat after you. Then show them how to spell *fa, fe, fi, fo,* and *fu*. For item 7, read the words aloud and have students match each word on the left with a word on the right that means the opposite.

Ff

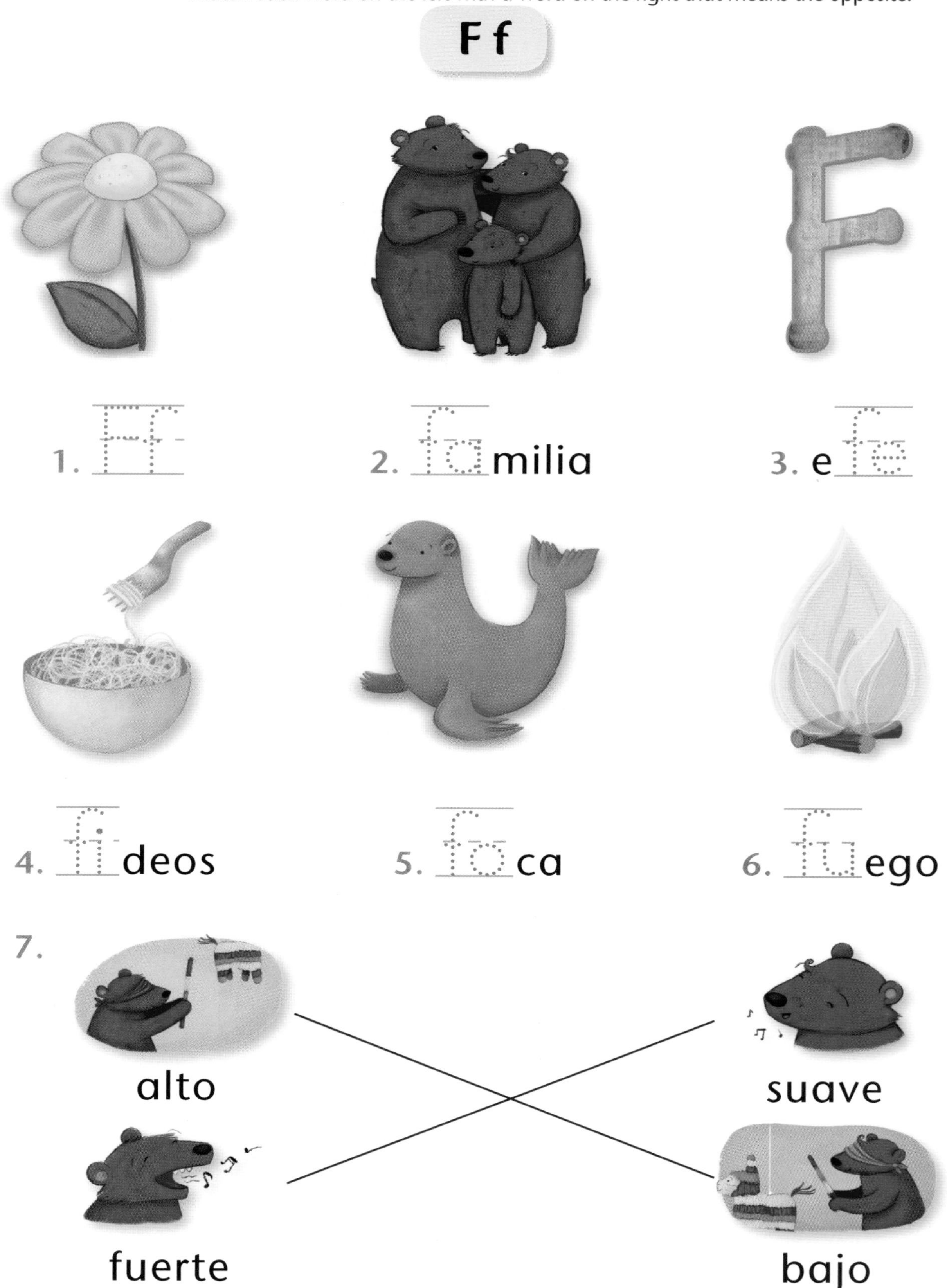

Así se escribe

Explain that words like *él*, *ella*, *ellos*, and *ellas* are used in place of the nouns, and are called pronouns. Help groups of students model these pronouns. For items 1–3, read the sentences and have students complete each word by tracing the missing letters. Then read the names in each sentence and the pronouns on the right, and have students match the pronoun with the right sentence.

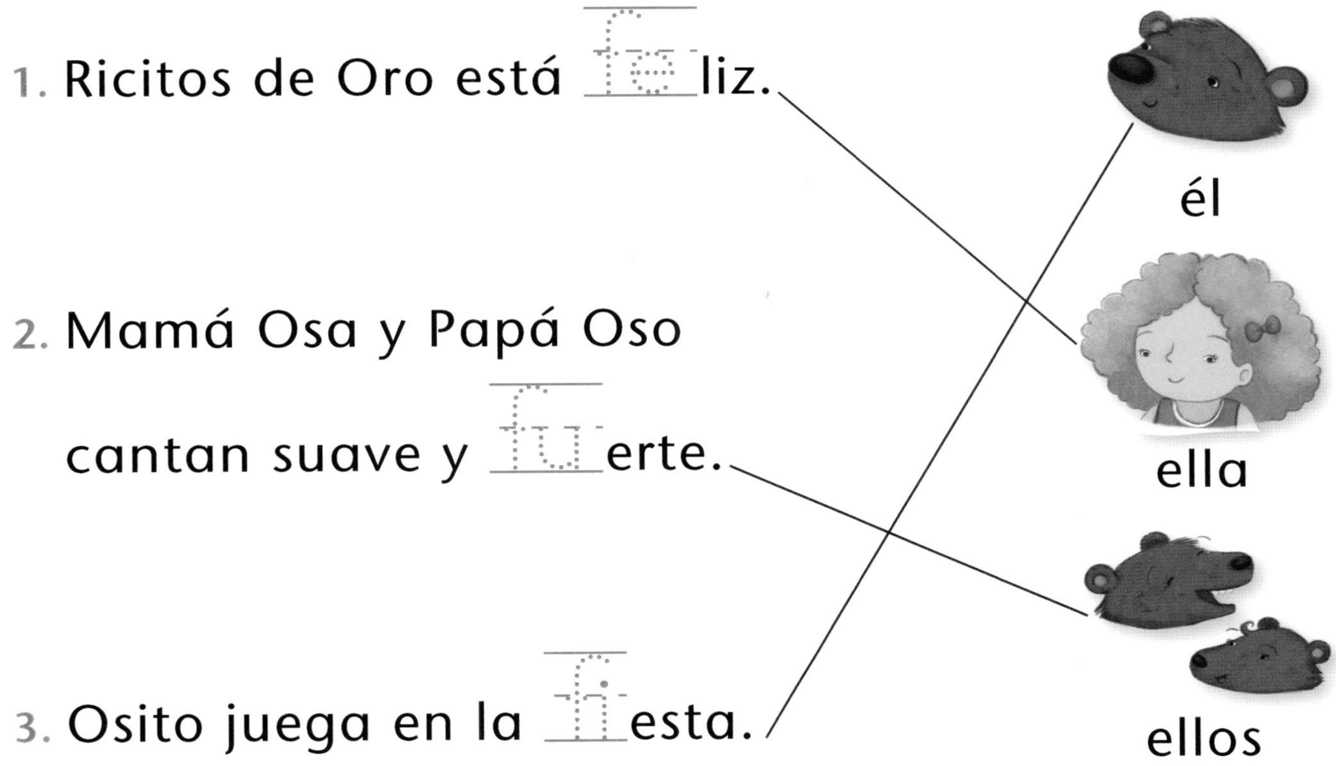

1. Ricitos de Oro está feliz.
2. Mamá Osa y Papá Oso cantan suave y fuerte.
3. Osito juega en la fiesta.

él

ella

ellos

A escribir

Review story vocabulary and the syllables *fe* and *fi*. Read the question and the sentence and have students write the missing letters. Discuss some of the things students do to celebrate their birthday. Then have them complete the second sentence by drawing two things they do to celebrate their birthday, in the order in which the events take place.

- ¿Cómo celebramos el cumpleaños?

Ricitos de Oro juega y canta feliz en su fiesta de cumpleaños.

Yo ______ y ______.

Answers will vary.

Discuss how to introduce friends in Spanish and the different ways friends can communicate with each other. Ask: *¿Cómo presentamos a un nuevo amigo?* How do you introduce a new friend? *¿Cómo nos comunicamos con nuestros amigos?* How do we communicate with our friends?

Read the title of the story and the author's name. Then have students view the illustrations and help them "read" them. Explain that the children in the pictures are communicating with each other using sign language because one of them is deaf. Elicit other ways Jacobo could communicate with others, such as writing notes and sending emails.

Te presento a Jacobo

Amy White
adaptación

—Niños, les presento a Jacobo —dice la señora Pérez—. Es un alumno nuevo.
—¡Mucho gusto, Jacobo! —dicen todos.
—¿Qué hace Jacobo? —pregunta Jesús.

Read the text aloud several times and have students read along with you. Emphasize the Spanish *j* sound as you read the words *Jacobo* and *Jesús*. Explain that the Spanish *j* sound is similar to the English *h* sound. Next have students use vocabulary from the story to ask questions about Jacobo and his friends. Have pairs of students take turns asking and answering questions.

—Jacobo se comunica con señas —dice la señora Pérez—. Él es sordo. No puede oír. Pero entiende cuando le hablan. Él lee los labios de las personas.

Discuss new vocabulary. Then help students identify important events in the story, such as *La maestra presenta a Jacobo, Jacobo conoce a Jesús y a Maricela,* and *Jacobo enseña a sus amigos a hablar con señas.* Have students retell the story by sharing these events in the order in which they occurred.

—¿Nos enseñas a hablar con señas? —dice Maricela.

—Sí —dice Jacobo con sus manos.

Jesús y Maricela aprenden una nueva forma de hablar.

¡Es divertido tener nuevos amigos!

Comprendo lo que leí

Discuss the selection and help students complete the activities on the answer sheets. For items 1–2, have students circle the correct answer. For item 3, have students number the pictures to show the order of events in the story. Then have pairs of students take turns retelling the events.

1.

a. Puede oír.

(b.) Habla con señas.

2.

(a.) Aprenden señas.

b. No pueden oír.

3.

2

1

3

Así se dice

For item 1, point to the picture of Jacobo and say his name. Then show students how to write the letter *J j*. For items 2–6, point to the pictures as you say the words. Have students repeat after you. Then show them how to spell the syllables *ja, je, ji, jo,* and *ju*. For item 7, read the words and have students match them with the correct illustration on the answer sheet.

J j

Así se escribe

Explain that names of people are spelled with capital letters. For items 1–2, read the sentences and have students trace the words that complete the sentences. Contrast the use of capital and lowercase letters.

1. El nuevo alumno se llama Jacobo.
2. En el recreo, Jacobo y Jesús hablan con señas y juegan.

A escribir

Review story vocabulary. Read the question and the sentence and have students write the missing word. Then have students complete the second sentence by drawing themselves as they communicate with a friend. Finally, have students communicate with a partner in the manner they described in their picture.

- ¿Cómo nos comunicamos?

Jacobo se comunica con señas.

Yo me comunico ______. Answers will vary.

Discuss different kinds of clothes. Ask: *¿Qué ropa usan?* What clothes do you wear? *¿Cómo es su ropa?* What do your clothes look like?

Read the title of the story and the author's name. Then have students view the illustrations and help them "read"them. Explain that the story is about a proud emperor. Elicit that an emperor is like a king. Encourage them to guess what may have happened to the emperor's clothes.

La ropa del emperador

Hans Christian Andersen
adaptación

El emperador es muy rico y poderoso.
Pero no es muy inteligente.
Un día, un vendedor va a la casa
del emperador.

Read the text aloud several times and have students read along with you. Emphasize the hard *c* sound as you read the words *casa, camisa, compra,* and *camina.* Explain that the letter *c* sounds like *k* when it is followed by the vowels *a, o,* or *u.* Next have students use vocabulary from the story to ask questions about the emperor and the salesman. Pairs of students take turns asking and answering questions.

—Tengo una ropa especial —dice el vendedor—. Sólo las personas honestas pueden ver esta ropa. El emperador no puede ver el pantalón ni la camisa. ¡Pero el emperador compra la ropa!

Review new vocabulary. Then discuss the main theme in the story. Remind students that it is about a man who was so proud that he ended up making a fool of himself. Elicit from students why they think the emperor was so proud. Ask them to think about a time when they may have been too proud themselves and encourage them to share their experiences.

—Quiero que la gente vea que soy
honesto —dice el emperador.
Luego camina por la ciudad con su ropa nueva.
¡La gente ve que el emperador no tiene ropa!
Todos piensan que es muy tonto.

Comprendo lo que leí

Discuss the selection and help students complete the activities on the answer sheets. For items 1–2, have students circle the correct answer. For item 3, have students complete the sentences by drawing what the emperor thinks of himself (that he's a wise man), and what others think about him (that he's a fool).

1.

(a.) Compra la ropa.

b. Camina por la ciudad.

2.

a. Es inteligente.

(b.) Es tonto.

3. El emperador piensa ________.

La gente piensa ________.

Answers will vary.

Así se dice

For item 1, point to the picture and say the word *casa*. Show students how to spell the letter *C c*. For items 2–4, point to the pictures as you say the words. Have students repeat after you. Then show students how to spell the syllables *ca*, *co*, and *cu*. For item 5, read the words and have students circle the words for items of clothing.

C c

1. C c

2. ca misa

3. ca ma

4. co rona

5. co pa

6. cu chara

7. camina | camisa | emperador

pantalón | compra | casa

Así se escribe

Explain that there are words that express an action, such as *caminar*, *comer*, *comprar*, and *correr*. For items 1–2, read the sentences and have students trace the action word that completes each sentence. Then have them draw the emperor doing each action.

1. El emperador compra la ropa.

Drawing should show the emperor buying clothes.

2. El emperador camina por la ciudad.

Drawing should show the emperor walking.

A escribir

Review story vocabulary. Read the question and the sentence, and have students write the missing word. Then have students complete the second sentence by drawing the clothes they usually wear to school. Finally, have students share their writing with a partner.

- ¿Qué ropa usamos?

El emperador usa una  camisa y un pantalón.

Yo uso  .

Answers will vary.

Vamos a aprender
Descubre República Dominicana

Discuss school supplies and books. Ask: *¿Qué útiles usan en la escuela?* What supplies do you use at school? *¿Les gustan los libros? ¿Por qué?* Do you like books? Why? *¿Para qué sirven los libros? ¿Por qué?* What are books good for? Why?

Read the story title and the author's name. Then have students view the illustrations and help them "read" them. Explain that the images show books through different times in history. Ask: *¿En qué se parecen estos libros a los que ustedes leen?* How are these books similar to yours? Encourage students to show their own books as they respond.

Los primeros libros

Patricia E. Acosta

Los primeros libros eran de barro.
¡Los libros de barro eran muy delicados!

Algunos libros eran de papiro.
El papiro sale de una planta.
¡Los rollos de papiro eran muy largos!

Read the text aloud several times and have students read along with you. Emphasize the *d* sound as you read the words *lodo, delicados, madera, duros,* and *digitales*. Then read the text again. Help students make inferences by asking: *¿Por qué creen que los libros de barro eran delicados?* Why do you think clay books were delicate? Elicit or explain that clay books were fragile. Have students pretend to read fragile clay books, long scrolls, heavy wooden books, light paper books and e-books.

Otros libros eran de madera.
La madera sale de los árboles.
¡Los libros de madera eran muy duros y pesados!

Review new vocabulary. Remind students that they compare things when they say how they are alike. Then explain that they can contrast things by saying how they are different. Ask students to explain how the books described in the text are similar and how they are different from each other. Encourage them to use clues from the images and the reading.

Ahora los libros son de papel.
El papel sale de los árboles.
Otros libros son digitales.
¡Los libros de papel y los digitales son muy útiles!

Comprendo lo que leí

Discuss the selection and help students complete the activities on the answer sheets. For items 1–2, have students circle the correct answer. For item 3, read the captions and have students draw their favorite book. Finally, have students say one thing that is the same and one thing that is different about the books.

1.

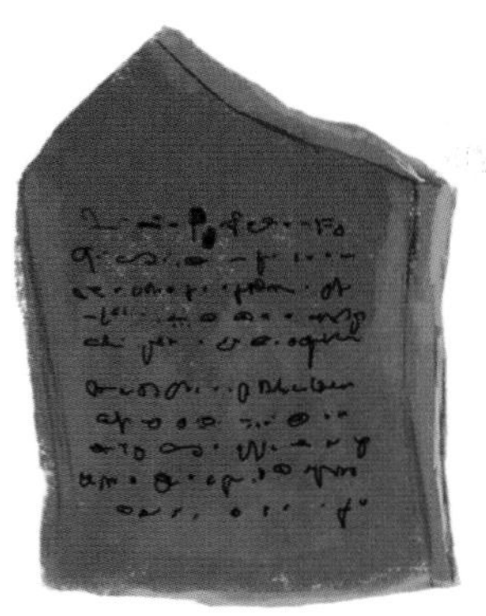

(a.) Es de barro.
b. Es de papel.

2.

a. Es de papiro.
(b.) Es de madera.

3.

papiro

mi libro

Answers will vary.

Así se dice

For item 1, point to the picture and say the word *dedo*. Show students how to spell the letter *D d*. For items 2–6, point to the pictures as you say the words. Have students repeat after you. Then show how to spell the syllables *da, de, di, do,* and *du*. For item 7, read the phrases aloud and have students match each one with the correct illustration on the answer sheet.

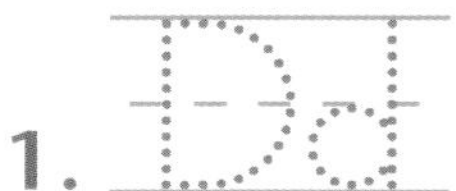

1. Dd
2. da ma
3. ma de ra

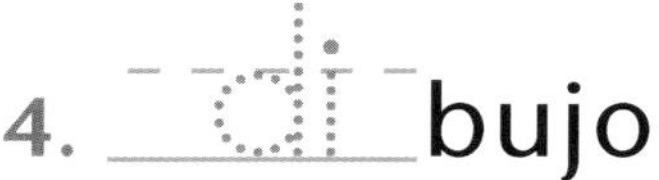

4. di bujo
5. lo do
6. du na

7.

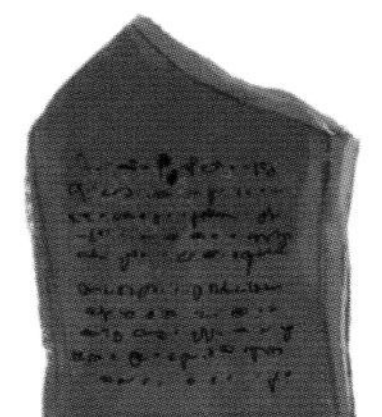

libro digital | libro de papel | libro de barro

Así se escribe

Explain that descriptive words tell us about things, people, animals, and places. For items 1–3, read each sentence and have students trace the descriptive words. Explain that these descriptive words tell us about the books. Then read the sentences again and have students match each sentence with the book it describes.

1. Es largo.
2. Es duro.
3. Es delicado.

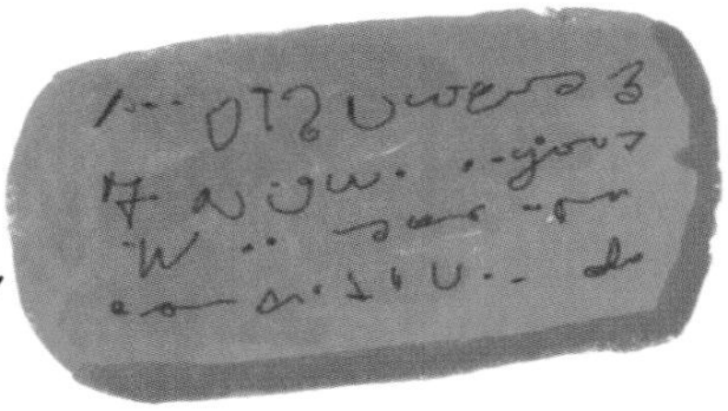

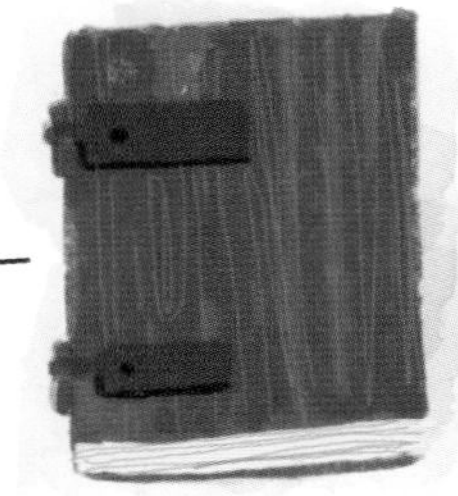

A escribir

Review story vocabulary. Read the question and the sentences and have students write the missing word. Then discuss the kinds of books we now have. Have students complete the second sentence by drawing two of their books. Then have students compare their books with those of a partner.

- ¿Cómo son los libros?

Antes los libros eran de barro.

Ahora mis libros son ______.

Answers will vary.

Discuss different ways animals communicate. Ask: *¿Cómo se comunican los animales?* How do animals communicate with each other? *¿Por qué necesitan comunicarse los animales?* Why do animals need to communicate?

Read the title of the story and the author's name. Then have students view the illustrations and help them "read" them. Explain that all honeybees have jobs. Then tell students they will learn how dancing is part of a scout honeybee's job.

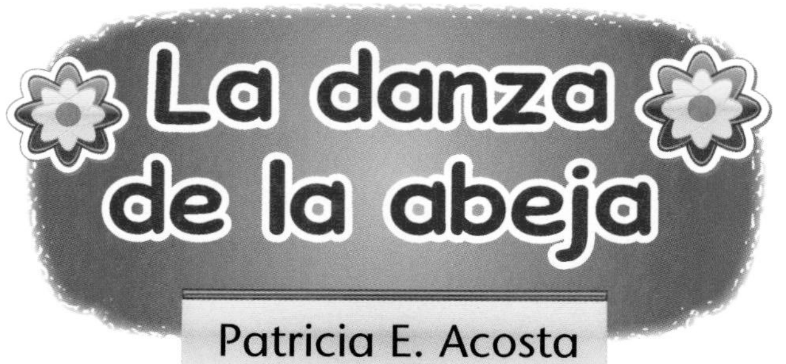

La danza de la abeja

Patricia E. Acosta

La abeja exploradora se comunica con una danza. Su danza les dice a otras abejas dónde hay alimento.

Read the text aloud several times and have students read along with you. Review sequence by having students retell what happens *primero* and *después*. Emphasize the *t* sound as you read the words *también*, *alimento*, and *está*. Then explain position words like *cerca* and *lejos* by having students move closer to and farther from each other.

Primero, la abeja exploradora busca el alimento. Después, ella vuela a su colmena. En la colmena viven otras abejas. Ellas también quieren saber dónde hay alimento.

Review new vocabulary. Read the story again and elicit that the text is about how some bees dance to communicate with others. Review important facts in the text and have students demonstrate the dance of the bee. Finally, elicit sources where they could find out more information about the dance of the bees, such as science books and the Internet.

La abeja exploradora danza en un círculo. Eso dice que el alimento está cerca.

La abeja también danza con su pancita. ¡La mueve de lado a lado! Eso dice que el alimento está lejos.

Comprendo lo que leí

Discuss the selection and help students complete the activities on the answer sheets. For items 1–2, have students circle the correct answer. For item 3, review important details about how the bees communicate. Then have students draw an important detail from the reading.

1.

ⓐ alimento
b. colmena

2.

a. La abeja camina.
ⓑ La abeja danza.

3.

Answers will vary.

Así se dice

For item 1, point to the picture and say the word *tortuga*. Then show students how to spell the letter *T t*. For items 2–6, point to the pictures as you say the words. Have students repeat after you. Then show them how to spell the syllables *ta, te, ti, to,* and *tu*. For items 7–8, read the words for the location of food for the bees. Then have students circle the correct answer on the answer sheet.

T t

1. Tt

2. tarántula

3. serpiente

4. tigre

5. toro

6. tucán

7. cerca  lejos

8. (cerca) lejos

Así se escribe

Point to the exclamation marks and explain that to express a strong emotion we use an opening exclamation mark (¡) at the beginning and a closing exclamation mark (!) at the end of a sentence. For item 1, read the sentence and have students trace the exclamation marks. For item 2, read the sentence and have students add exclamation marks.

1. ¡Se mueve de lado a lado!

2. ¡Qué bonita danza!

A escribir

Review story vocabulary. Read the question and the sentences and have students write the missing word. Then discuss how different animals communicate, and have students complete the second sentence by drawing an animal of their choice and then drawing how the animal communicates, such as by barking, singing, or wagging its tail.

- ¿Cómo se comunican los animales?

La abeja se comunica con una danza. 

se comunica

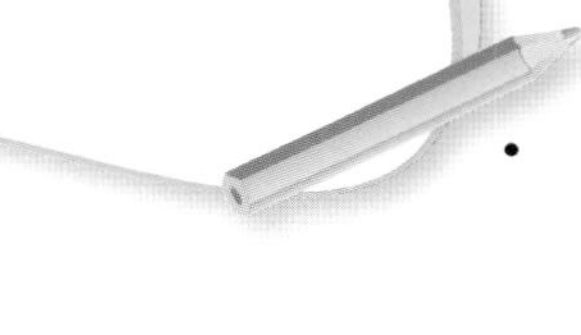

.

Answers will vary.

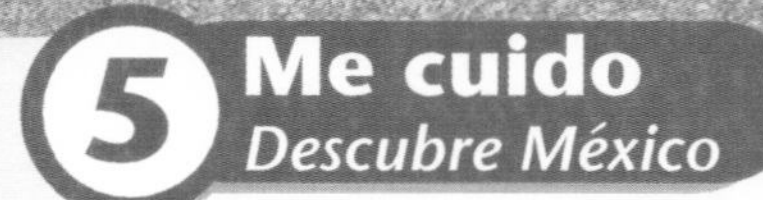

Discuss the five senses (*vista, olfato, gusto, tacto,* and *audición*) and why they are important. Ask: *¿Cuáles son los cinco sentidos?* What are the five senses? *¿Por qué es importante poder ver, oír, gustar, oler y sentir?* Why is it important to be able to see, hear, taste, smell, and feel?

Read the title of the story and the author's name. Mention that Amado Nervo is a very famous Mexican poet. Then have students view the illustrations and help them "read" them. Discuss which of the five senses each character is using.

Los sentidos

Amado Nervo

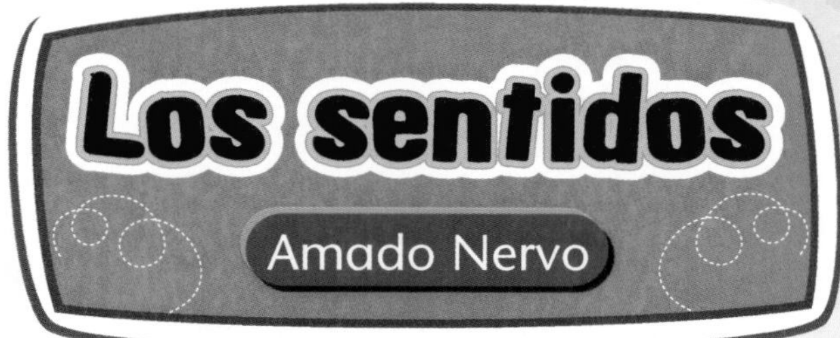

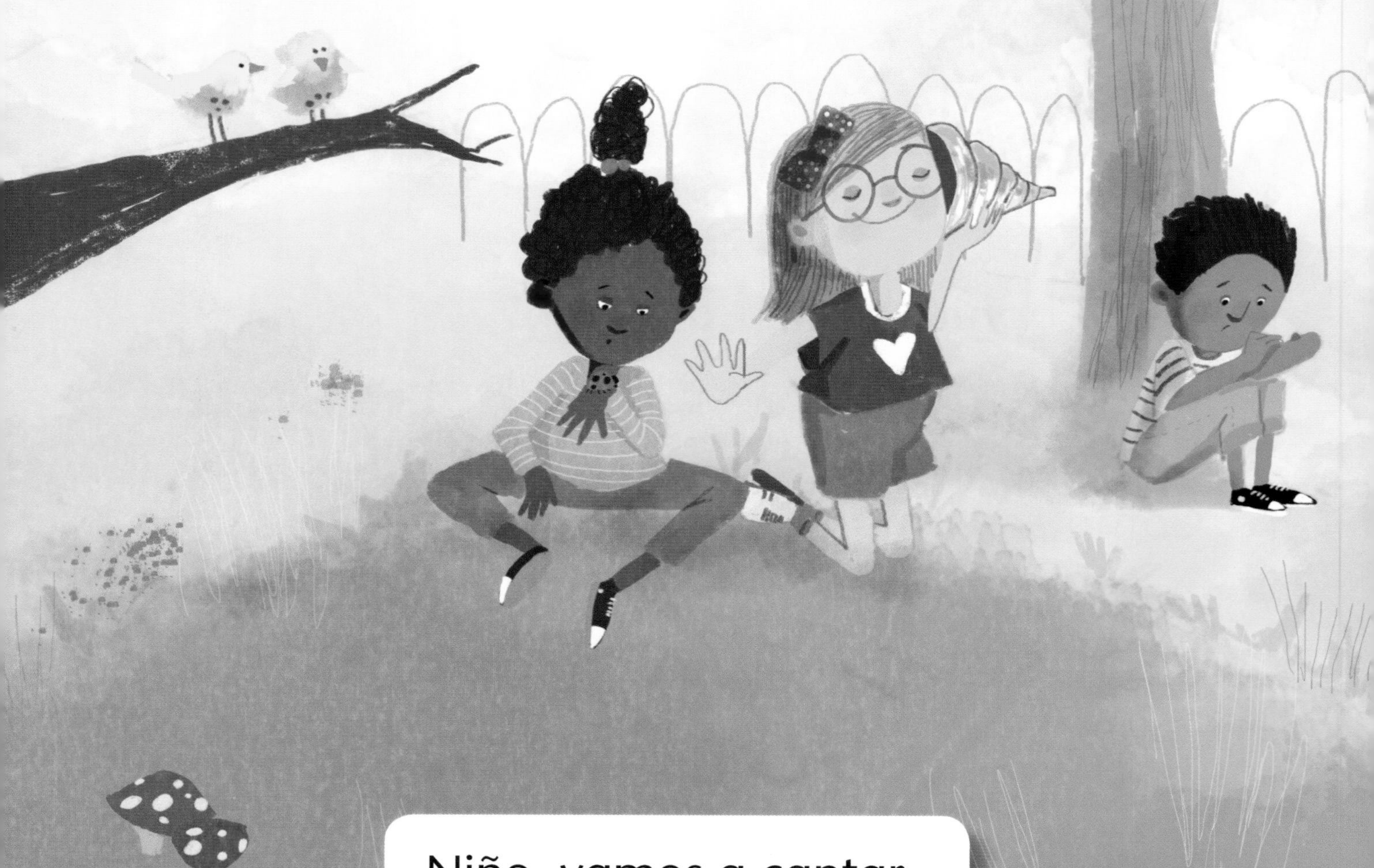

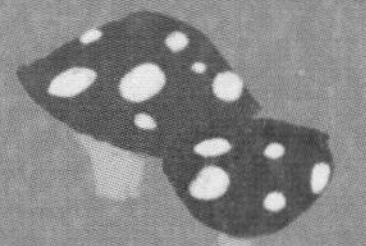

Niño, vamos a cantar
una bonita canción;
yo te voy a preguntar,
tú me vas a responder:

Read the text aloud several times and have students read along with you. Point out the words *qué* and *querer*. Write them on the board and have students repeat. Explain that in Spanish a *u* that follows a *q* has no sound, and that the form *qu-* always sounds like the English *k*. Then play the audio of the poem and have students repeat the lines as they sing along. Encourage them to point to their eyes, hands, ears, mouth, nose, and heart as they sing along.

—Los ojos, ¿para qué son?
—Los ojos son para ver.
—¿Y el tacto? —Para tocar.
—¿Y el oído? —Para oír.

Review new vocabulary. Tell students that all stories and poems have a narrator, or a person who tells the story. Explain that when the narrator is a character in the story, he or she often uses the word *yo*. Read the poem again and ask students how they can tell the narrator is a character in this poem. Finally elicit sources where they could find out more information about the five senses, such as science books and the Internet.

—¿Y el gusto? —Para gustar.
—¿Y el olfato? —Para oler.
—¿Y el alma? —Para sentir,
para querer y pensar.

Comprendo lo que leí

Discuss the selection and help students complete the activities on the answer sheets. For items 1–2, have students circle the correct answer. For item 3, read the first stanza again. Then have students mark an X on the picture that shows who the author is talking to in the poem.

1.

a. Son para oler.
(b.) Son para ver.

2.

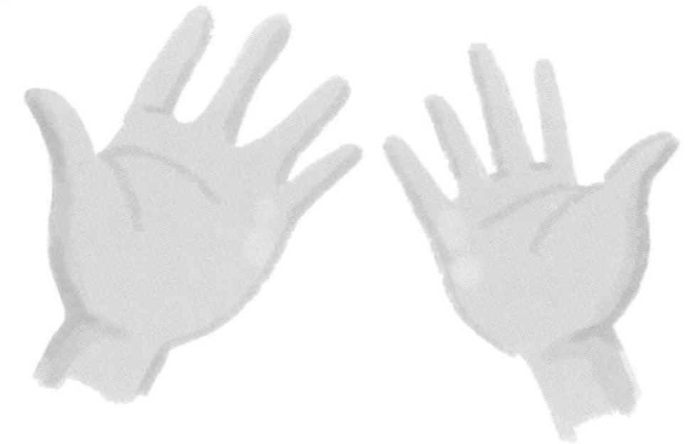

(a.) Son para tocar.
b. Son para oír.

3.

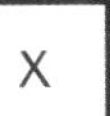

X

not marked

Así se dice

For item 1, point to the picture and say the word *queso*. Show students how to spell the letter *Q q*. For items 2–4, point to the images as you say the words. Have students repeat after you. Then show them how to spell the syllables *que* and *qui*. For item 5, read the words aloud and have students match the word with the correct illustration on the answer sheet.

Que que **Qui qui**

1. Qq

2. parque

3. mantequilla

4. mosquito

5.

Así se escribe

Tell students that sometimes we can create new words when we add or change a syllable. For items 1–3, have students read the words on the left and orally separate them into syllables. Then have them trace the words on the right. Finally read the words on the right and discuss with students how the words have changed.

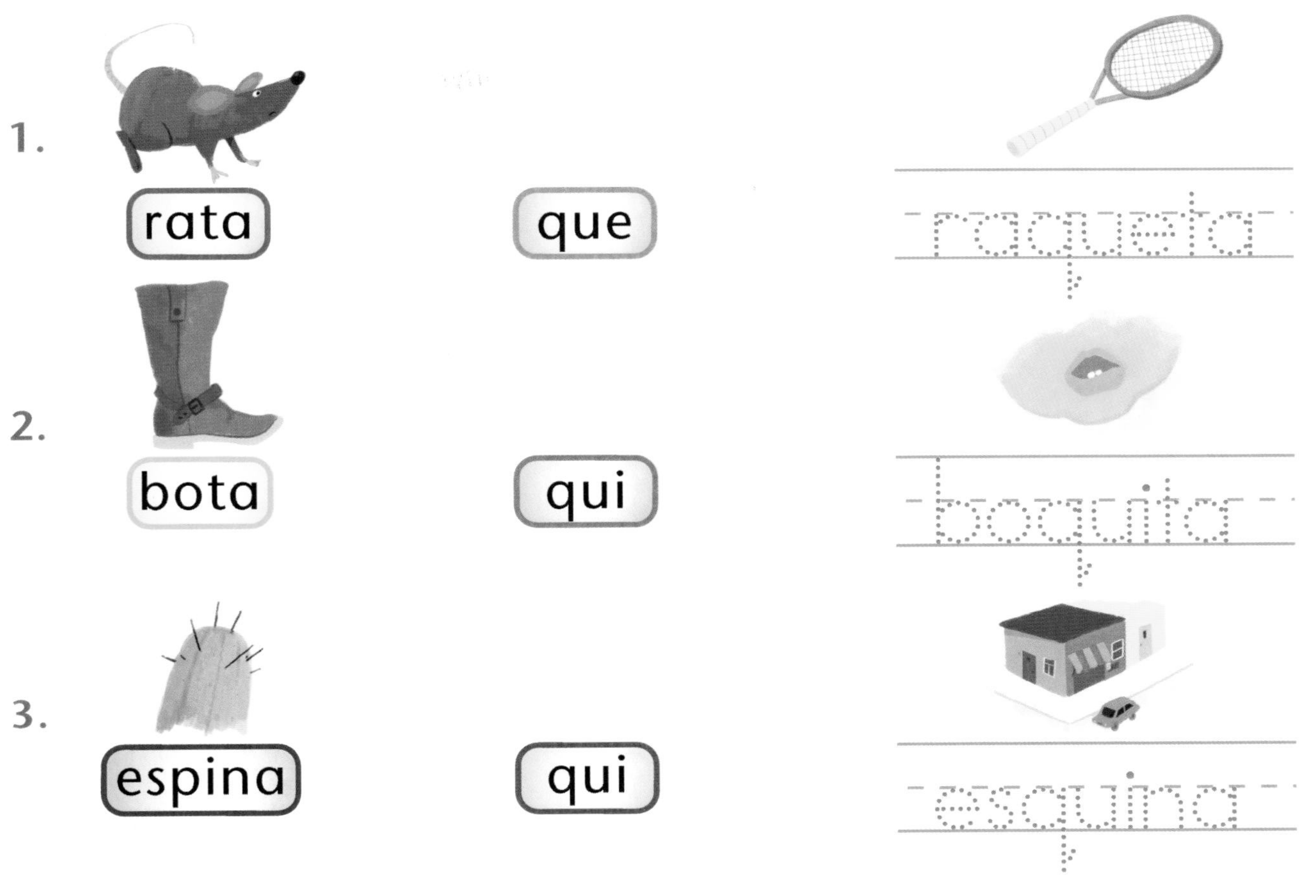

A escribir

Review story vocabulary related to the senses. Then read the question and the sentence. Ask students to complete the next sentence by saying what the sense is and what it is used for (e.g., *El tacto es para tocar*). Help students revise and edit their sentences on their answer sheet. Finally ask students to draw the body part related to that sense.

- ¿Para qué son los sentidos?

  El tacto es para tocar.

  ______________ es para ______________.

Answers will vary.

Discuss the weather. Ask: *¿Les gustan los días soleados? ¿Por qué?* Do you like sunny days? Why? *¿Les gustan los días lluviosos? ¿Por qué?* Do you like rainy days? Why? *¿Prefieren el frío o el calor?* Do you prefer cool or warm weather? Read the title of the songs. Then have students view the illustrations and help them "read" them. Elicit or explain that one day is sunny (*soleado*) and the other day is rainy (*lluvioso*).

El lagarto y la lagartija,
van juntitos a tomar el sol,
en invierno cuando hace frío,
en verano cuando hace calor.

Read the lines aloud several times and have students read along with you. Emphasize the hard *g* sound in the words *lagarto* and *lagartija*. Then play the audio of the songs and have students repeat the lines as they sing along. Encourage them to "shiver" when they say the word *frío* and to fan themselves when they say *calor*. You may also have students hold hands and dance in a circle as they sing along.

Si el cielo está gris,
no quieren salir.
Si el cielo está azul,
van derecho a la luz.

Review new vocabulary. Elicit or explain that the *ll* has a sound similar to that of the letter *y*. Then have students compare and contrast the scenes depicted in both poems by asking them how the characters, the place, and the weather are alike and how they are different.

Ya lloviendo está

tradicional

Ya lloviendo está.
Ya lloviendo está.
Plin, plin, plin, plin.
Ya lloviendo está.

Comprendo lo que leí

Discuss the selection and help students complete the activities on the answer sheets. For items 1–2, have students circle the correct answer. For item 3, read the headings and explain that they refer to the two scenes depicted in the poems. Have students compare and contrast the scenes by drawing two things that are different on each side and one thing that is alike in the middle.

1. 

(a.) Hace calor.
b. Hace frío.

2. 

a. Hace sol.
(b.) Está lloviendo.

3.

soleado | lluvioso

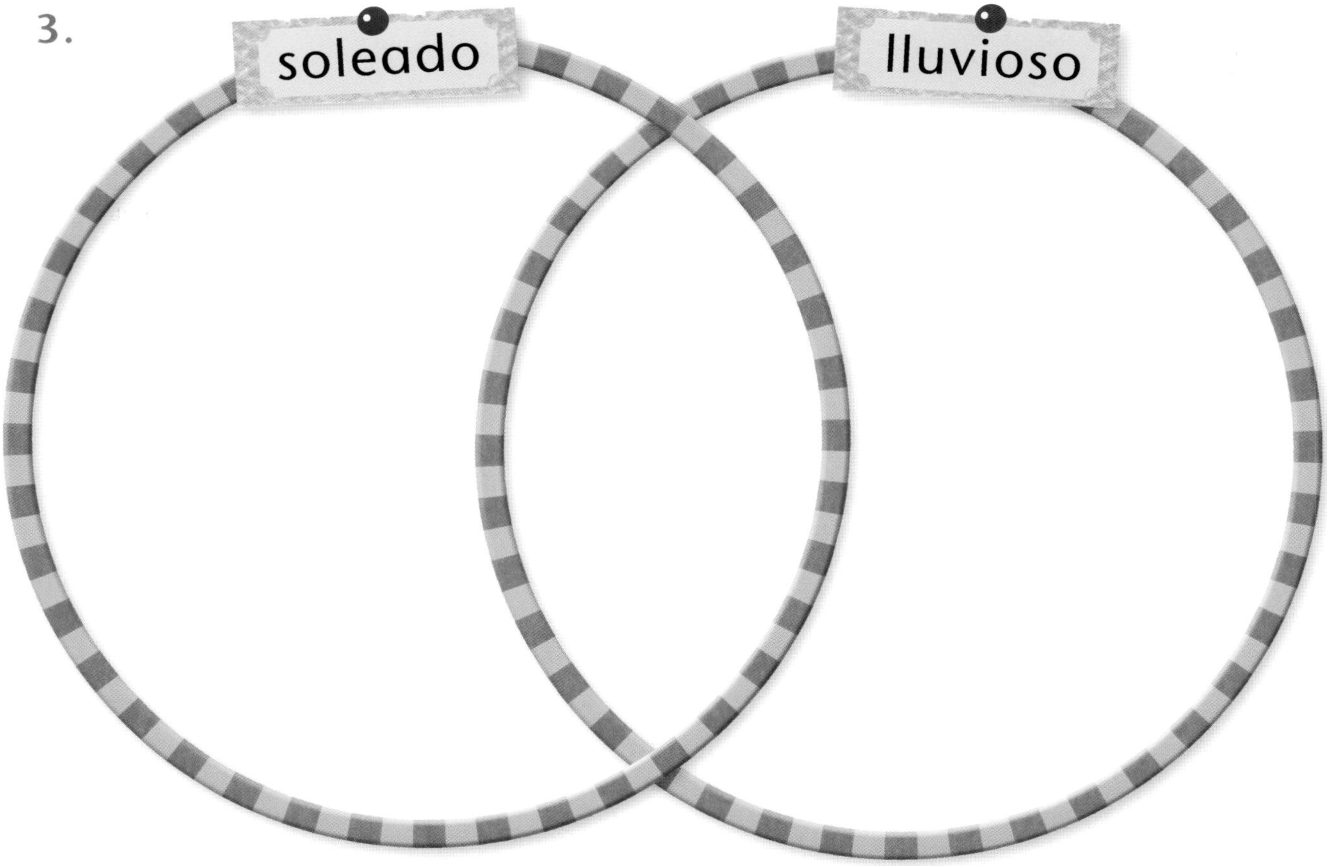

Answers will vary.

Así se dice

For item 1, point to the picture and say the word *gato*. Show students how to spell the letter *G g*. For items 2–4, guide students in spelling the syllables *ga*, *go*, and *gu*. For item 5, have students observe the illustrations and read the captions along with you. Then have them match the words on the right with the correct scene.

Ga ga **Go go** **Gu gu**

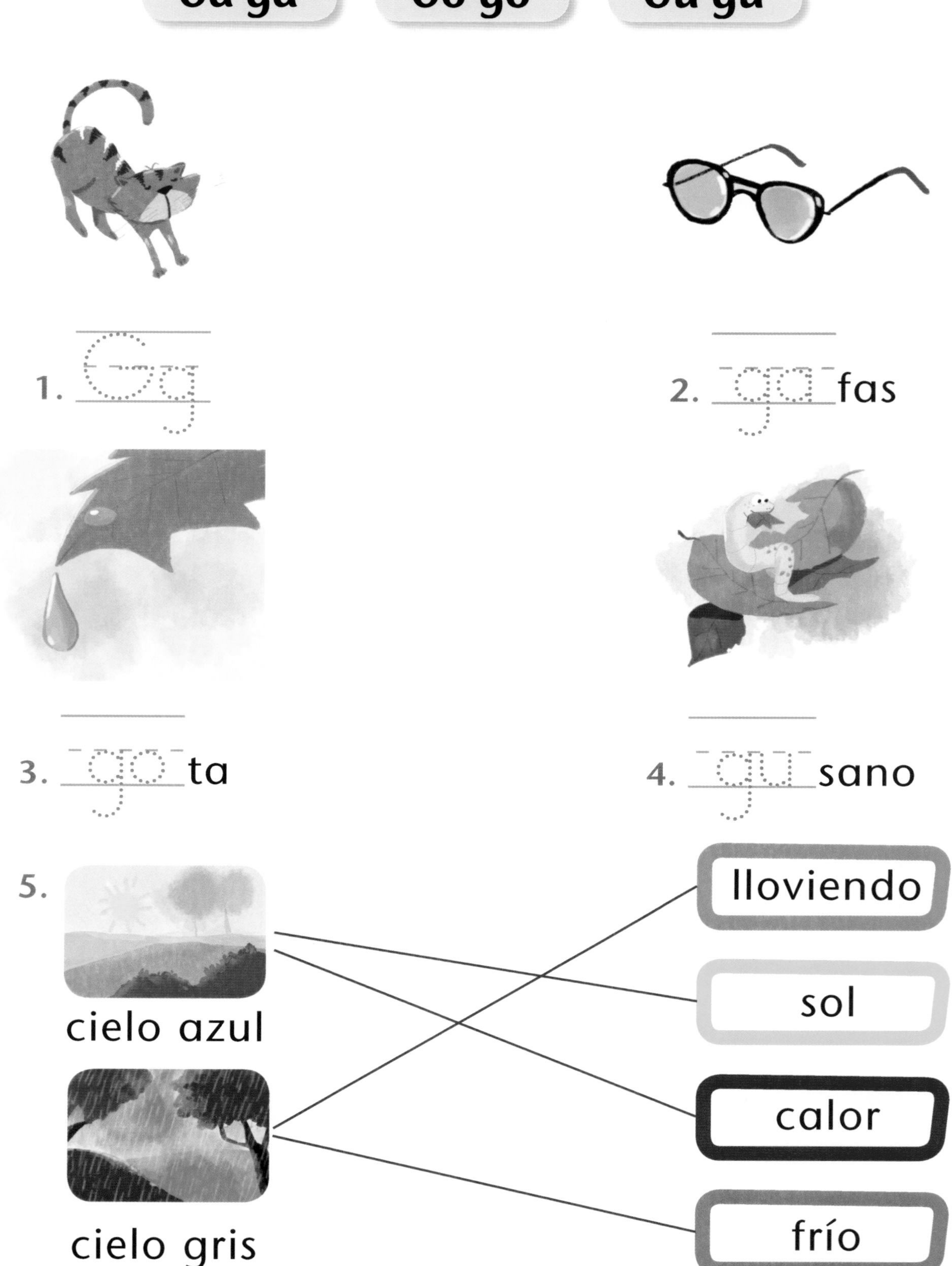

Así se escribe

Explain that words such as *a* and *en* tell us where someone or something is and when something happens. For items 1–2, discuss the pictures and have students trace the names for the animals in the first blank. Then read the sentences and have students complete them by tracing the preposition.

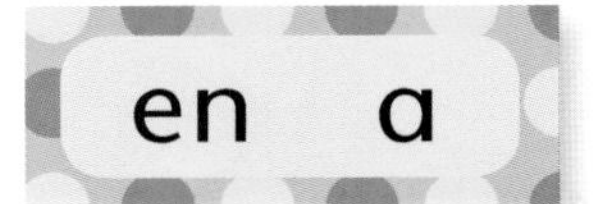

1. El lagarto va a tomar el sol.

2. La lagartija no quiere salir

en invierno.

A escribir

Review story vocabulary. Read the first question and the first sentence, and have students complete it. Then read the second question and the second sentence, and ask students to complete it by writing in the blank whether they like hot or cold weather, and by drawing one thing they like to do in that kind of weather. Assist students as needed. Encourage them to share their work.

- ¿Prefieres el frío o el calor? ¿Por qué?

Yo prefiero ______________________.

Answers will vary.

Cuando hace ______________________ yo,

Answers will vary.

Discuss famous sports professionals. Ask: *¿Qué deportes les gustan?* What sports do you like? *¿Quién es su jugadora o jugador favorito? ¿Por qué?* Who's your favorite player? Why? *¿Qué saben sobre su jugadora o jugador favorito?* What do you know about your favorite player?

Read the title and the author's name. Then have students view the illustrations and help them "read" them. Tell students that they will read the biography of a famous Panamanian baseball player. Explain that a biography (*biografía*) is the story of someone's life.

Mariano Rivera

Oswaldo Portillo

Mariano Rivera es un jugador de béisbol muy famoso.
Él es uno de los mejores lanzadores del mundo.
Mariano lanza la pelota muy rápido y con mucha fuerza.
¡A veces la pelota rompe el bate del otro jugador!

Read the text aloud several times and have students read along with you. Emphasize the *b* sound in the words *béisbol, bate, árboles,* and *también.* Then choose a few two- or three-syllable words from the story, such as *ju-ga-dor, pe-lo-ta,* and *ba-te,* and help students orally separate them into syllables. Have them pretend to throw a baseball every time they say a syllable.

Mariano nació en Panamá. Allí aprendió a jugar béisbol.
Mariano y sus amigos no tenían bates ni guantes de béisbol.
Ellos hacían bates con las ramas de los árboles.
También hacían guantes con cajas de cartón.

Review new vocabulary as you demonstrate how to use the illustrated glossary to find the meaning of unfamiliar words. Then help students to identify and organize the main events in the text and have them retell the story of Mariano Rivera in their own words. You may also encourage them to tell their own stories.

¡Ahora Mariano tiene muchos premios de béisbol!
A él le gusta ganar premios. Pero también le gusta ayudar.
Él ayuda a otros jugadores a aprender inglés y español.
Él también ayuda a construir iglesias y escuelas para los niños en Panamá.

Comprendo lo que leí

For items 1–2, have students circle the correct answer. For item 3, review the main events in the life of Mariano Rivera. Then have students draw an event of Rivera's childhood in the left box and an event of his life as an adult in the right box. Finally, have students use their drawings to retell the story of Mariano Rivera.

1.

a. Nació en Nueva York.

(b.) Nació en Panamá.

2.

(a.) Es lanzador.

b. Es bateador.

3.

Students should draw an event from Rivera's childhood.

Students should draw an event from Rivera's life as an adult.

Así se dice

For item 1, point to the picture and say *béisbol*. Show students how to spell the letter *B b*. For items 2–6, point to the images as you say the words. Have students repeat after you. Then show them how to spell *ba, be, bi, bo*, and *bu*. For item 7, read the words with students and then have them circle the words that are related to the game of baseball.

B b

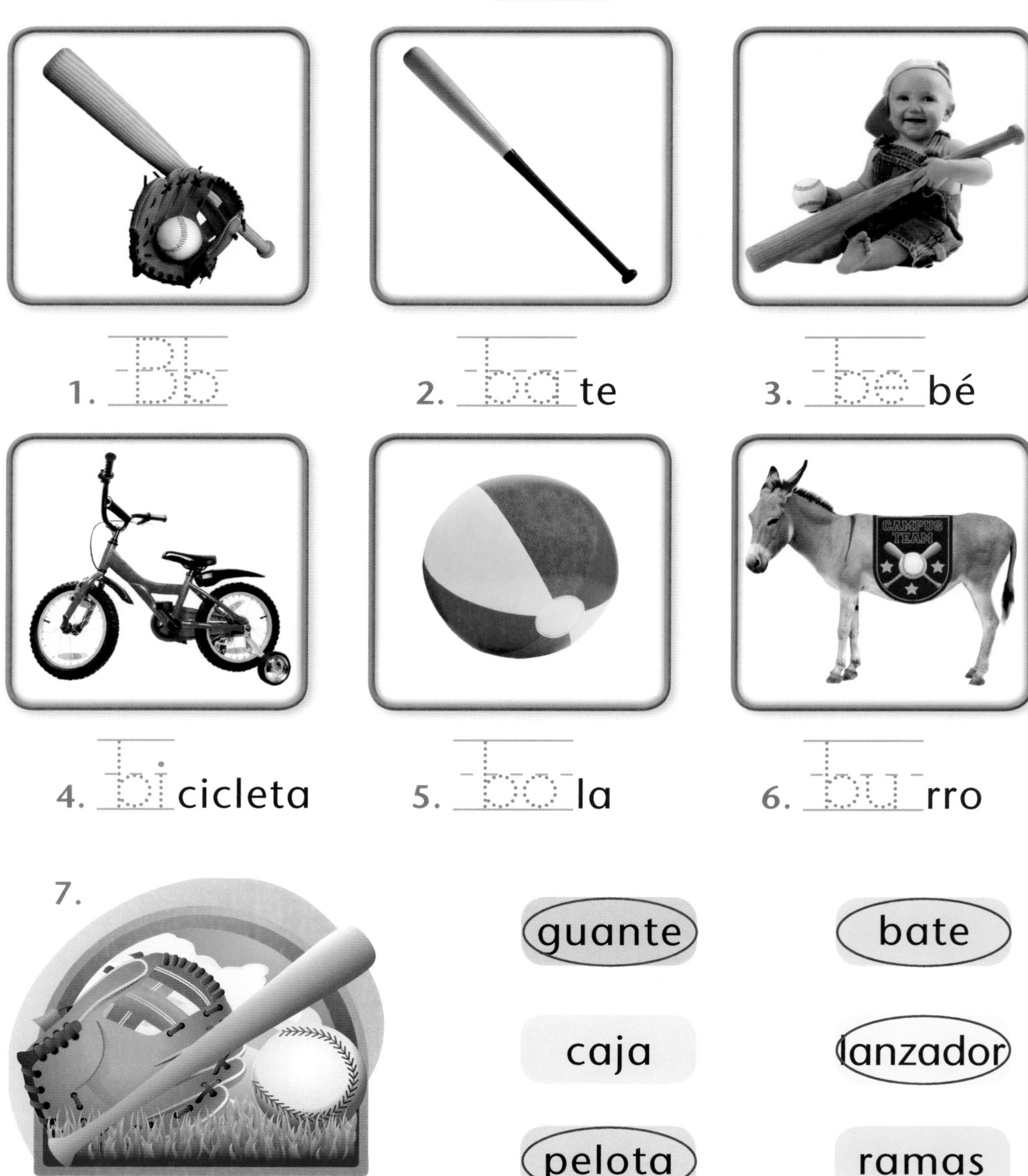

Así se escribe

Ask students to observe the pictures and read the captions along with you. Explain that words such as *él* and *ellos* are used in place of words that name people and are called pronouns. For items 1–2, have students trace the missing words. Then have them identify the pronouns.

él

ellos

1. Mariano Rivera es jugador de béisbol.

   Él es un jugador muy famoso.

2. Mariano y sus amigos no tenían bates.

   Ellos no tenían guantes.

A escribir

Review the story of Mariano Rivera. Read the question and help students complete the sentences by writing their name and hometown. Finally ask students to think of two important events in their lives to include in their own stories, and have them draw them in the order in which they happened. Help advanced students to write a sentence describing each event.

- ¿Quién eres?

Yo soy ______. Nací en ______.

Answers will vary.

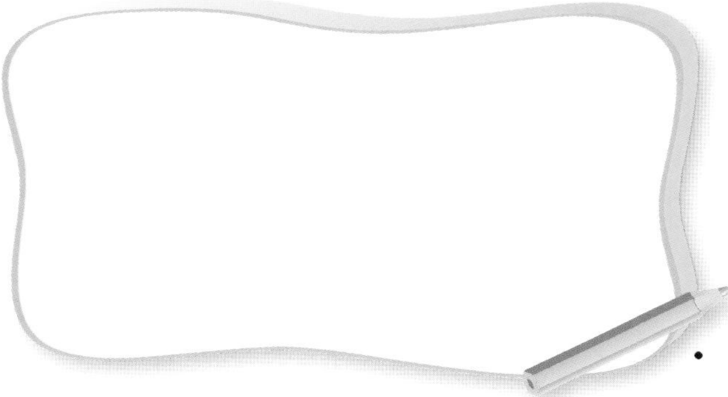

Answers will vary.

Discuss Mother's Day celebrations. Ask: *¿Les gusta celebrar el Día de la Madre? ¿Por qué?* Do you like to celebrate Mother's Day? Why? *¿Cómo celebran el Día de la Madre?* How do you celebrate Mother's Day? Read the title and the authors' names. Then have students view the illustrations and help them "read" them. Elicit that Mother's Day is celebrated in all Spanish-speaking countries. Review the days of the week and months of the year, pointing out that Mother's Day is celebrated in the United States on the second Sunday in May, and on different dates in other countries.

El Día de la Madre

Patricia E. Acosta y Mario Castro

Yo te canto a ti, mamita,
porque es tu día hoy.
Eres muy dulce y hermosa.
Por ti feliz yo soy.

Read the poem/song aloud several times and have students read along with you. Emphasize the soft *c* sound in the words *dulce* and *diciendo*. Remind students that the Spanish *c* has two separate sounds, hard and soft. Explain that in words with *ce* and *ci*, the *c* sounds like an *s*. Then play the audio of the song and have students repeat the lines as they sing along.

Me gusta cuando sonríes.
Cuando me abrazas, mamá,
siento como que me estás diciendo
que tú siempre me amarás.

Review new vocabulary. Remind students that all stories and poems have a narrator who tells the story, and when the narrator is also a character he or she often uses the word *yo*. Read the poem/song again and ask students how they can tell the narrator is a character in this poem. Finally help students orally create their own rhymes. You might have them dictate their rhymes to you as you write them on cards for their moms.

Hoy te canto a ti, mamita,
y alegre cantaré
porque tú eres mi madre,
y siempre te amaré.

Comprendo lo que leí

Discuss the selection and help students complete the activities on the answer sheets. For items 1–2, have students circle the correct answer. For item 3, explain that the phrase *yo te canto a ti, mamita* shows the narrator is telling the story. Then read the sentence starter and have students be the narrator of their own story by drawing themselves saying or doing something for their mom on Mother's Day.

1.

(a.) Es hermosa.
b. Es famosa.

2.

a. Yo te abrazo.
(b.) Yo te canto.

3. Yo

Answers will vary.

Así se dice

For items 1–5, point to the images as you say the words. Have students repeat after you. Then show them how to spell the syllables *ce* and *ci*. For item 6, read the words aloud and have students match each word with the correct illustration on the answer sheet.

Ce ce **Ci ci**

1. ce real

2. dul ce

3. ci ruela

4. bi ci cleta

5. ce lebración

6.

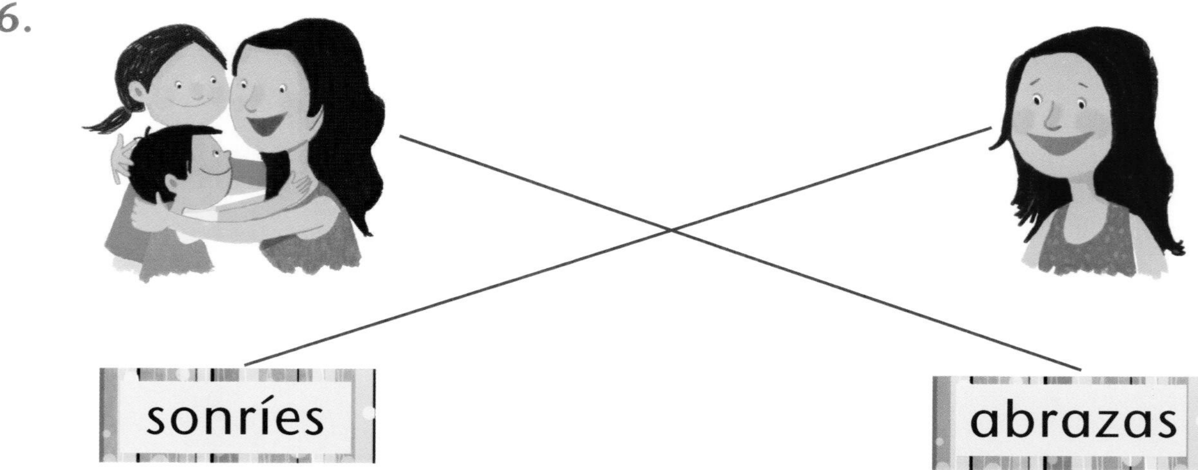

Así se escribe

Remind students that descriptive words tell us about things, people, animals, and places. For item 1, read the sentence and have students trace the descriptive words that complete it. For item 2, read the words and explain what they mean. Then read the sentence and have students complete it by choosing and writing down one of the descriptive words.

1. Mamá eres muy 

y hermosa.

2. alegre | amorosa | bonita | paciente

Mamá te quiero porque eres ________________.

Answers will vary.

A escribir

Review story vocabulary. Then read the question and discuss some of the things students do to celebrate Mother's Day. Explain that they are going to write a rhyme on a card for their mom. Encourage them to come up with their own words or use the ones from the previous activity. Assist them as necessary. Finally, have students decorate their card.

- ¿Cómo celebramos el Día de la Madre?

Answers will vary.

abeja
bee

alimento
food

animal
animal

abrazo
hug

alumno
student

aprender
to learn

afuera
outside

amiga
friend (girl)

árbol
tree

alegre
happy

amigo
friend (boy)

arquitecto
architect

B

barco
boat

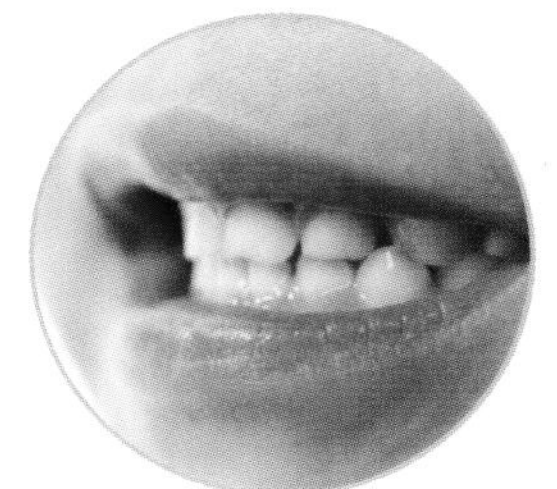

boca
mouth

cantar
to sing

barro
clay

C

calor
heat

capitán
captain

béisbol
sport of baseball

caminar
to walk

cepillar
to brush

bigote
mustache

camisa
shirt

cerca
near

choza
hut

comprar
to buy

dentista
dentist

cielo
sky

construir
to build

desayunar
to eat breakfast

colmena
bee hive

cumpleaños
birthday

dibujar
to draw

comer
to eat

D

danza
dance

E

edificio
building

escalera
stairs

escultora
sculptor

flor
flower

escribir
to write

estaciones
seasons

frío
cold

escritor
writer

F

feliz
happy

G

gato
cat

escuela
school

fiesta
party

guante
glove

gusto
taste

hermosa
beautiful

isla
island

H

hablar
to talk

hocico
snout

J

jabón
soap

hermana
sister

hoja
leaf

jugar
to play

hermano
brother

I

invierno
winter

L

lanzar
to throw

lanzador
pitcher

libro
book

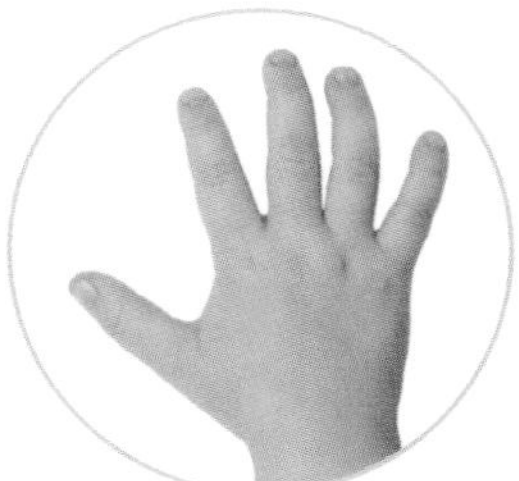

mano
hand

lavar
to wash

llover
to rain

médico
doctor

leer
to read

madera
wood

mosquito
mosquito

lejos
far

maestro
teacher

mover
to move

nadar
to swim

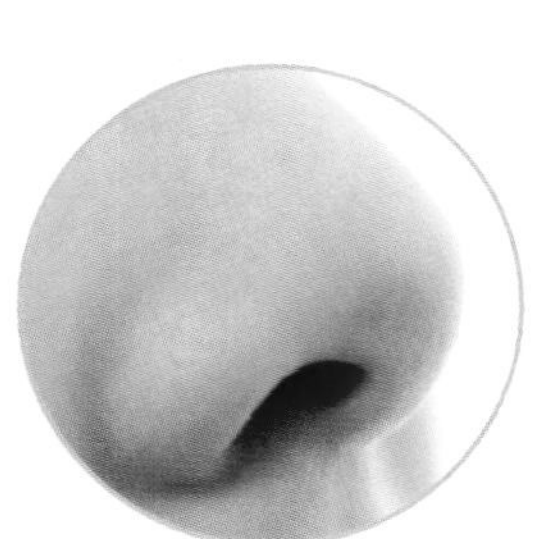

nariz
nose

navegar
to sail

nieve
snow

niños
children

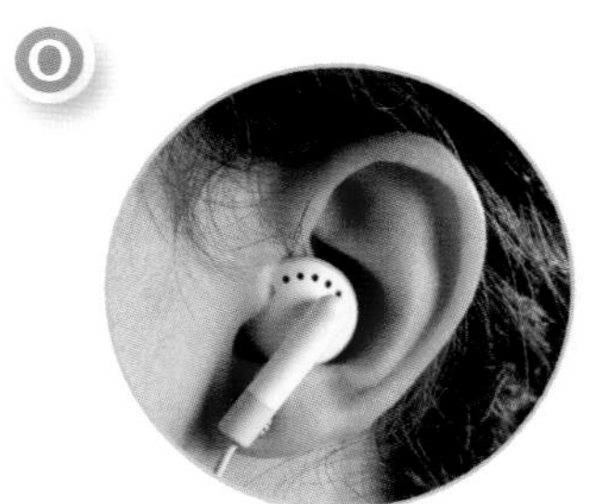

oído
ear

oír
to hear

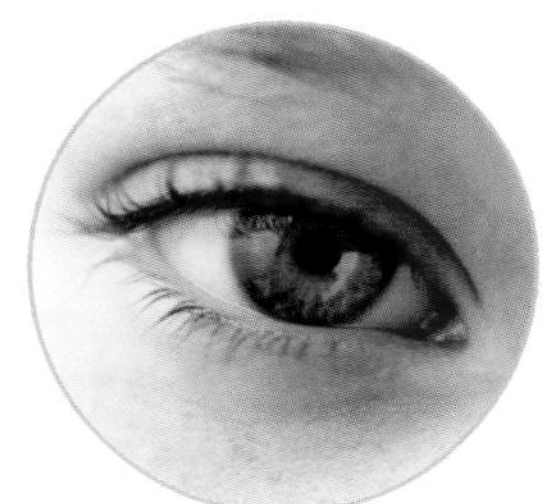

ojo
eye

oler
to smell

oreja
ear

otoño
fall / autumn

pantalón
pants

papel
paper

pequeño
small

planta
plant

papiro
papyrus

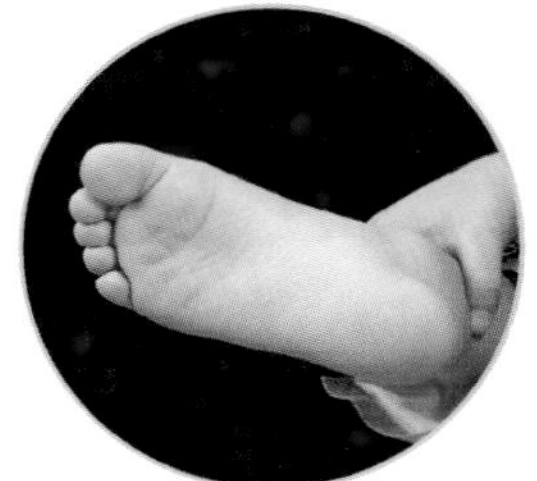

pie
foot

premio
award

peinar
to comb

pintar
to color or paint

presentar
to introduce

pelota
ball

pintora
painter / artist

primavera
spring

R

rabo
tail

ropa
clothes

semana
week

rama
branch

S

salón de clase
classroom

seña
sign

rata
rat

saludable
healthy

sol
sun

ratón
mouse

sapo
toad

sonreír
to smile

suave
soft

ver
to see

T

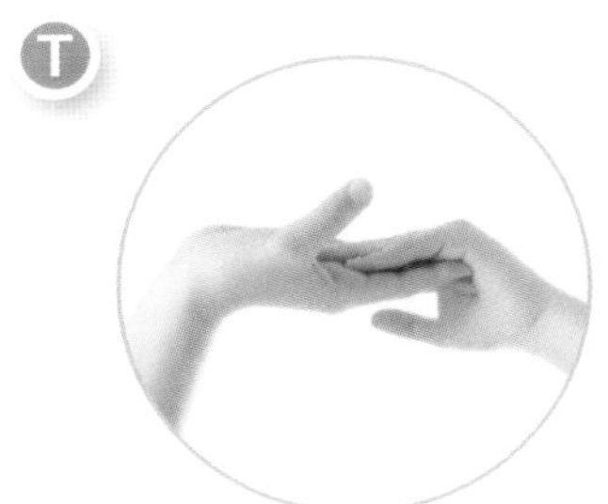

tacto
sense of touch

verano
summer

tocar música
to play music

veterinaria
veterinarian

V

vendedor
salesman

Los números

1
uno

2
dos

3
tres

4
cuatro

5
cinco

6
seis

7
siete

8
ocho

9
nueve

10
diez

11
once

12
doce

Los colores

amarillo(a)
yellow

marrón
brown

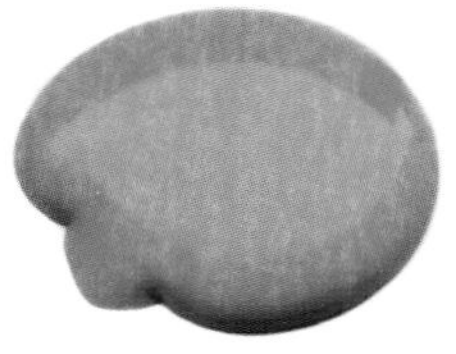

verde
green

azul
blue

negro(a)
black

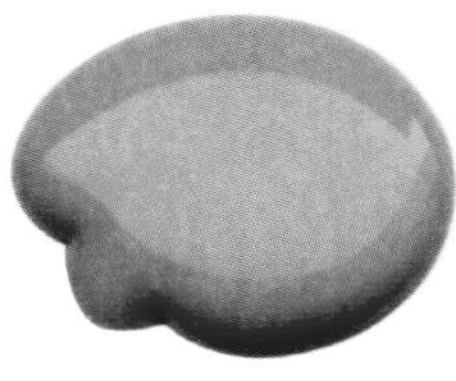

anaranjado(a)
orange

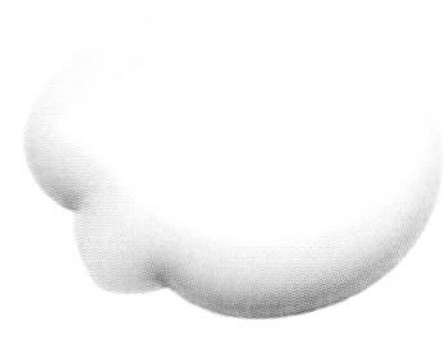

blanco(a)
white

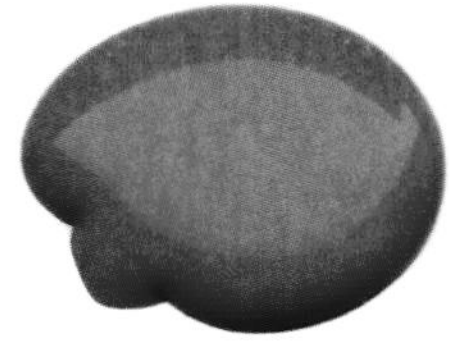

rojo(a)
red

morado(a)
purple

rosado(a)
pink

gris
grey